D1366397

Pieces of Night

David W. Elliott

Pieces of Night

A Novel of Childhood

Holt, Rinehart and Winston

New York   Chicago   San Francisco

For Jo
For Teddy
For Children

Pieces of Night

I

The first thing I remember as a child is feet. There were always two of them, both on me and on the others in the big bed. I was about three at the beginning of my memory and my crib was at the foot of that bed and either the room was tiny or my father was tall or both because I remember reaching through the bars many times to touch his toes. But father didn't sleep at home very much. I know this not from an absence of feet; there were always lots of them to touch on that bed, mother hated to sleep alone; but with him I had merely to reach out my fingers, and with all the others, the much shorter ones, both in height and in temper, I sometimes had to reach all the way out with my arms to make that touch.

Our apartment in East Haven, Connecticut, had five small rooms. It was reached after kindergarten and first and second grades by walking many blocks and up three flights of outdoor wooden stairs that still creak and sway in my memory. The door at the top was always a screen one. (Could it be I only lived there in summer? But no, because I remember once getting hit in the face with a snowball.) And I remember the door was always locked as if mother was trying to tell me something, but that the hook could be lifted with something in my hand that was slim and silver. Beyond that door, which opened to the kitchen, there was sometimes a lunchtime sandwich or, if not, a tiny red box or two of raisins in the cupboard, or at least some sugar in a yellow tin can that lived so high on a shelf I would have to use a chair. After picking out the ants from the sugar, either dropping them tenderly to the floor or squeezing them red in my fingers depending on how my day had gone, I would wipe my hands on my pants and eat. After, I would clean up carefully and put everything back and walk into the biggest room. There was a black shiny table there that spent all its time looking out a dirty window and across a narrow alley at another dirty window where there was another little boy who also sat at a black table that I suppose was shiny too. I saw him once, eating his breakfast just as I was doing, and at first I thought he was my reflection, but then I saw him smile. It was in the days before kindergarten and since I then never left the apartment I was shocked to find there were other people like me, small and naked and eating breakfast in the same world and at the same time. I looked for him a million times after that but I never saw him again.

Opposite my table was a yellow room with wet crumbling walls where the bathing was done. I don't remember a toilet being there, though I'm sure there had to be one, but hanging above my tub there was a long white string to a lamp that I pretended to touch many times, but almost never did for fear of being burned to ashes. The tips of my fingers and toes would always turn white and wrinkled in that tub under the string, and I think now that the reason mother kept me there so long was so she could pretend it wasn't me at all who was doing all that splashing, but instead one of her visitors. I could splash all

I wanted; I could pound on the water so hard it would get scared and jump to the floor. But if I ever said anything, even if only to the soggy bear I always took with me, she would yell at me to shut up and keep washing and not to touch that string. I was a very clean person in those days.

Toward the end of the bath I would begin to worry a little about my white and wrinkled toe and finger tips. I would examine them closely, always with excitement, and with the fear my body was rotting. Then mother would come in to lift me out, warning me again about the string, and while she was unplugging the plug with her back turned, I would reach way up to see how close I could come to death. But nothing ever happened.

The pleasure of people's feet was nothing in comparison to the long and hard toweling that mother would then give me. I would already be happy at not being ashes, and she would lift and carry me out and smack my wet feet on that black shiny table and attack my body from head to wrinkled toe. She never liked me, though I never thought of that then, but she must have been in love with my body. I think now that maybe it was the same with all her other visitors.

Only when my body was a deep red all over would she consider me done and then lift me off the table to the dirty floor and fold her towel and go away without a word. This is what I remember most about her: she seldom spoke to anyone. When she had gone, I would see that my toe and finger tips were smooth again and as red as the rest of me and I would be happy at the thought I wasn't going to rot away after all. I would spend a long time admiring the footprints I had left on the table, and lift up one foot at a time to see if it had really been me who had made them. Then I would slowly rub them out toe by toe.

I loved my body then because she loved it, but I liked little else about the rest of me. I thought my face was cute because her visitors kept saying it was, and sometimes even to me. I liked my long brown hair because they would always laugh whenever I shook my head to make it fall in front of my eyes. But I remember very well how much I hated it when they messed it up with their big hands. And more than most other things I loved the way my feet became black on the floor within minutes after the bath. I would take one step and look at the back foot and then take another step and look at the other foot, and I would do this dozens of times, each time being more amazed at the dark changes the world could make on a person with each step. Also I loved the middle of me for the way it swelled with food or with air or with the pride of owning the only black feet in the house. But very early on I learned that such small things didn't matter much, and I began to see that I was something of a joke; the visitors would laugh no matter what I said or how long it had taken for me to say it, and mother would tell me to shut up and go away someplace whenever I stepped into her bedroom doorway, and the one with her at the time would laugh for a long time. Then I would run. And the more I would try to figure things out by running as fast as I could around the black table, the louder the visitor would laugh, not stopping until the joke was exhausted.

I was naked almost all the time in that apartment, but unlike the visitors I was never wrapped in a sheet. But I guess one wouldn't have stayed on me anyway. Looking like ghosts, as I thought then, or like Romans in white togas, as my memory would say when I was old enough to know about Romans, the visitors would walk around in their sheets and I would play a game with them they never knew about. I would stare at their faces when they weren't looking and then try to picture them in my mind long after they'd gone so that when they came back I would know them. But they never did come back a second time and the picture in my mind was always wrong. But I kept playing my game anyway. It was easy since even after I had grown too big for the crib and just right for an army cot in the hallway where the busy front door was, I did most of my running and playing in the room of the black table through which they all had to pass to get to the bedroom door that was always open.

When I got to be old enough, I was allowed to play the much better game of going on errands to the liquor store that was downstairs and just around the corner. I used the front stairs for this, and not the outside wooden ones, and I remember being very proud of my trips. I pretended each time that I was the man who was going to drink from those pretty bottles in brown paper, those bad-smelling bottles that always seemed to make everyone a little happier than they were. And I pretended that when I got home, there would be no one there except mother, and that instead of waking up in darkness as I did sometimes, listening to the squeaky voice of the front door-knob, the footsteps and heavy breathing, the clinking and laughter of glasses and strangers, the metal on metal of bed-springs grinding, the rattle of snores and the blacker sleep of dreaming worse things, that the large woman with the powerful voice when she used it and the hair like the mane of a lion was waiting only for me to touch that hair, only for me to listen to her whispers in our darkness of tiny sounds that would last all night long until the sun sang at our window and I had to go to school.

I awoke one day to a further promotion. I think I was about five or six and either in kindergarten or first grade. Next to the liquor store there was a bar where people could go when they didn't have anybody to visit, or when if they did they had to wait their turn. It was always so dark in there I could never see anyone unless they came up real close. Bumping into chairs and people I would go all the way to the back, as I'd been told to do, and there I would stand in a corner next to a wet table and wait. A great many years later, and while standing quietly in other bars in other towns, the thick smoke would swirl around me and never once get into my eyes, and I would think it funny it had hurt so much at one time. There was a loud music box with red and green lights (there would always be one like that in my future bars too), and with my eyes blinded by the red and green smoke and with my ears hearing nothing because of the noise, I would wait for someone to call my name. Unlike the long waits of later years, someone eventually would, but I could never hear what they were trying to say to me, not even when they bent down to yell, so whenever I found myself being yelled at I would say as loud as I could—it's okay now, you can come up.

The visitor would then laugh and follow me, or I would follow him; they always seemed to know the right direction, and I remember that even in the clean air I still wouldn't be able to see or hear too well and sometimes the visitor would have to take me by the hand so I wouldn't wander off into traffic.

There was only one time when I brought up a visitor who wasn't welcome. As we were going up the outdoor wooden stairs, he stopped me on the second floor and kissed me on top of the head, which I thought was funny. There was a couch on that floor with flowers all over it and sharp silver springs; our downstairs neighbors sat on it when the weather was nice. The visitor sat down and told me to sit beside him and as I played with one of the springs that was poking out of a flower, he played with my knee, and I thought that was funny too, but all I could think of to say was—it's okay now, you can come up. And he did too, he came all the way up, and the unzipping of my pants rasped through the night and turned on the porch-light of the neighbor who slammed her head out of her window to yell at the visitor running down the stairs and me running up the stairs much louder than I'd ever heard a lady yell before. I don't remember what happened after that, probably nothing, but I do remember thinking the only one that liked me had to go.

One week, when I was in the second grade, and the only real reason I remember it is because Halloween came during that week, the traffic slowed and then died, and I was out of a job. I remember I asked mother why it was she no longer sent me down to get visitors and her only answer was—the boredom's set in.

But before the boredom set in I had been to the bar downstairs so often that the people in it, the ones I couldn't see, became quiet each time I walked in and turned on a fan each time to blow the smoke from my eyes, and I always felt very important, not knowing, as I would figure out years later, that no one ever saw I was there, except of course for the one who was waiting for me, and that there wasn't any fan, I was only getting used to the noise and the smoke.

I think it was the man who kissed me who was the cause of my being fired. But since almost all the visitors, both the ones I brought up and the ones who found their own way, are all jumbled up in my mind as one big lump, I can't really remember if he was at the tail-end of my trips or somewhere in the middle or even if perhaps he was the very first lucky one. But anyway, and for whatever reason, my job was over and mother's boredom was set in real deep. And for the first time that I could remember, the door to her bedroom would some-times be closed when I woke up in the morning and just as tightly closed when I came home because of lunchtime or be-cause the day was done and school was over. During the first few days I thought she was dead since she would never come out or make a noise even when I called to her to say good morning or good-bye or good night. But finally when she did come out a couple of times to go to the kitchen or the bathroom when she thought I wasn't looking, I would see the back of her dirty dress and would know she was still alive. But I remember such knowledge didn't mean very much, any more than I would care about the life or death of an ant I would catch stealing from my lunchtime yellow tin. Even later, after many days had gone by without that door opening at all, I felt nothing. It was when the moans started that I began to be afraid, that I began to want that door either to open for good or else weld itself sound-tight. Over the years since, I have been in and worked in many different hospitals in which there were closed doors where strange sounds were often shoved through the wood. But those sounds, to me anyway, always made some sense. I always had the feeling I'd been previously introduced to the patients, and that I knew perfectly well what it was they wanted and most of the time I would get it to them, or at least try to. But with mother and with the terrible sounds she made behind that door for an entire Halloween week and the week after, it was different. I could stand there and listen and even ask her what the matter was, but I couldn't open that door, partly because I'd never opened it before and had never seen it closed either, but mostly because it might just as well have been iron welded to iron since neither my feet nor my hands would move in any direction except away, no matter how loudly she moaned or how much I would want to get in. And it went on and on. The clock in my head that all schoolchildren have would wake me in the morning and as if she'd heard it too she would begin the day's moanings that I would say good-bye to and then hear again during my raisin or sugar lunch and again when school was done and there was no place else to go. At all three of these times I would walk around the black table with my clothes on for a change, and try my best to figure things out. I would sometimes feel the thick pieces of the welded iron trying to break apart in my mind, and I would want them to break, really I would, I would want to get to her not only to help but also to tell her that something was wrong with me too. But at the same time I would enjoy being alone, and the power and the dirt of doing with my clothes and body what I wanted, and the visitors being only in my mind, and especially the feeling that all the bad pain in the world was locked up real close where one could hear it and know it was there without being able to actually feel it. But sometimes at night, when the moanings were louder than any dream, I would wake up in the dark and feel funny inside, my first feelings of guilt, and think the world was gone, and I would get out of bed to touch things, familiar things like walls and doors and tables, and even though fully awake and walking around, I would fight against the dream I knew would come. And it always came, night after night and for many years after; head over heels and over and over, the men in my mind would somersault through the doors of a dead world and attack each other with feet while standing on heads. Then after a while, like everything else in life, the fighting would end and I would go back to bed and dream only of good things.

Halloween had slipped between the days of my life as mysteriously as everything else. One day it wasn't there and the next day it was. My class was told by our second grade teacher there would be a party that afternoon and we were all to find and put on costumes at home during lunchtime and wear them to school because it would be great fun not to be able to know who each other was. I went home and sat in the kitchen for a while, listening to mother moaning and trying to figure out where I could get a costume. I ate a box of raisins and then tore the empty box open and punched two eyes in the middle of it with a pencil. I found some string and tied it around the ends and put on the mask and went to school. All the way there I laughed to myself thinking no one would have a costume quite like mine. And I was right. I don't remember too many things about that school but I'll never forget the parade that rustled and beeped into the classroom where I was sitting in my red torn-up mask that had the word "raisins" between the eyes. One kid had on an Indian hat with bright feathers that hung to the floor. Another had on a sailor's uni-

form. Another wore a dress covered with buttons and a hand-
bag made out of someone's hair, which he kept opening and
closing like a mouth to make everyone laugh. And another
wore the baggy suit of a clown and had a horn in each hand
that he beeped all through the party. But the best of all was
some crazy girl who came dressed as a haystack. We put all the
chairs in a wide circle for the teacher to stand in the middle
of and point at each kid in turn to see if the rest of us could
guess his or her name. Except for the haystack and the kid in
the Indian hat, I was the only one whose name was known by
all and the only one to have a nickname, Raisins, for days afterward, until finally the air cleared and I was forgotten again
when some fat girl farted during a speech on the Constitution.

I remember only one other thing about that school. There
was a large dead tree at the end of the dirt play-yard that I
always went to during recess while the others played close to
the school. There was a black hole in the trunk of the tree and
inside on its soft floor were sawdust and leaves and bits of fur
some animal slept on whenever he knew I wasn't there. On the
rotting walls and hanging from the ceiling that went so dark
and so far into the tree that I could never see the end of it,
there were tiny spiders that stood quietly on webs as if waiting
for something to happen. I didn't know if they shared the home
with the animal or if they were only there to be eaten by it, sort
of like living iceboxes. But many times, before my own boredom set in, I brought raisins or pockets of sugar or pieces of

bread and put most of the food on the floor, hanging the small-est on the webs. And every time I came back the food would be gone and there would be big holes in the webs and I would try to imagine what the animal looked like and the more I thought of him the bigger he grew until in a few days he had grown so gigantic in my mind that he couldn't possibly have fit into such a small doorway. This confused me at first. I stopped bringing him food so he could lose weight. But he kept growing anyway. And he was fierce too, with long yellow teeth that hung over his chin and eyes so strong they could kill you just by looking at them. I began to tremble on the way to the tree. I began to feel, and not just to pretend, that I was in great danger. I would test my bravery by sometimes closing my eyes and sticking my arm in the hole real fast. But except for the webs that stuck to my fingers, nothing else ever happened; my arm would not come out a bloody chewed-off mess, and I would go back to school in happy disappointment. But one day I did see the monster. It was sitting on a thick branch and watching me. It was a chipmunk, and a very small one, and even more disappointing than my arm, which now would never have the chance to become a stump.

Halloween went. On the night of it I had tried to make another mask, this time using an old newspaper and with no words, only white space between the eyes. But the string kept tearing through the ends and I had to go to my first trick or treating in the same face I used every day. But I didn't mind too much. Nothing can hurt one on Halloween. Years later a friend of somebody I knew would lend me her kangaroo suit and I would go hopping down the street, barking at each door because that's what I thought kangaroos were supposed to do, nobody ever told me different, and even when some kids informed me I had no tail, that a kangaroo simply had to have a tail, I stayed happy anyway, thinking maybe another kangaroo had gotten hungry. And years after that, when I was about ten or eleven and living in a different world, I would travel down the street with a tough gang of kids and help them throw rocks at streetlights and through windows, and once we even tied a neighbor's clothesline clean around their house so they couldn't get out, and we barricaded a street with fallen trees and doll carriages and broken bicycles and little kids, and when the cops came we rose up out of the park and from behind statues and bushes to throw rocks and marbles and dirty words, and even though I would be so scared I would be shaking all over, I would still stay happy. Halloween was always like that, a day that nothing could hurt. Valentine's Day never meant a thing, mostly because I never got any cards. And birthdays and Christmases and Thanksgivings and Easters were always celebrated in the light, where anyone could see your face. But Halloween was strange and dark and free of all the rules and regulations the adults had written for us on some old paper somewhere to make us miserable on all the other days.

On my first Halloween, and on many of my others too, I forgot whoever was moaning at home and joined a group of kids who wouldn't even consider allowing me to join had it been daytime, or some normal night, or had they known how different I was from them. We went toward the light of each house, throwing rocks at the houses that had no lights, and we knocked on the doors and stood there knowing and silent with the greed-hungry mouths of our bags open so wide they could have swallowed a hippo apiece if by chance someone had one he wanted to get rid of. But whether it was a hippo, a penny, a gumdrop, or an entire Baby Ruth, we seldom said thank you or fuck you or anything because we knew whatever we got we owned: we had earned it during the previous three hundred and sixty-four days. But perhaps the thing I remember most is that we were always kind to each other on those cold nights, even if not on the day before or the day after. We were free of the real world, the one that made no sense, and we would form into little groups of strangers, the youngest of us making funny noises and bragging about our hauls, the oldest of us quiet and protective, directing the lost, inspiring the ones with empty bags, shouting quick warnings across the street whenever some-one was seen going up to a door where there was nothing to get, and examining our apples and oranges to check for slits that could mean there were razor blades inside.

I got one of those apples on my first Halloween and when I saw the blood on my fingers I told one of the big kids with us and he took it from me and lifted out the carelessly placed blade with such care it could just as well have been one of those papers the adults use to put rules down on. I remember we looked at it closely under a streetlight that made it shine red for a while and then green. The blade was old and rusty as if it had been saved over from last year. There was a name on it, but we quickly decided it was the company's and not the name of the person who had given it to me. The little kids thought it was funny, but the big ones got mad and told every other big kid they met that things like this shouldn't happen, not on Halloween, and that we should form into an army and march back on that house and tear it down. I tried to tell them I had forgotten just which house out of the many was the guilty one, but this unimportant fact bothered no one; the main thing was we were going to take that house apart brick by brick, smash the furniture, set fire to the dog, hang the cat, castrate the canary, mangle the mice, and other things like that. And we all meant it too, we really did. But the funny thing is, not one of us, not even in the safety of the dark, had found the courage to mention what he would do to the actual person who had given me the apple. I think about it now and I realize that even on Halloween we were scared stiff of adults, and totally defenseless no matter what they did to us.

One day the moaning stopped. It was after school and I was sitting on a chair in the kitchen eating the last of my Halloween presents, when right in the middle of a stale candy bar I suddenly got the feeling that my ears were clogged. I had become so used to the constant sound from the closed bedroom door that when it ended, I had the same lost feeling I would have years later when I would think my heart had given up. I stopped chewing and listened. I took another bite and then put the bar down and stood up. The chair squeaked. I heard a clock somewhere. One of our downstairs neighbors coughed, as if he too was afraid of the sudden silence. I tiptoed on loud feet to the door and I put my ear to it real close. At first I heard nothing except for the blood in my ear that was pounding against the wood. Then suddenly there was an explosion in my ear that made me jump back, and then another, and then a third. In the short time it took for the next three to hit me I realized that mother was knocking on the door in the one-two-three way she always did for luck whenever she was afraid, and that she was asking me in the voice of a mouse if it was all right to come out.

I don't remember what happened after that and I seldom try to. There have always been dark spaces in my mind whose purpose I guess is to keep some kind of order, to keep one memory separated from another so that they don't all start rotting together. And like missing teeth, they help me to appreciate the ones I do have, whether or not the ones remaining are worth saving.

But some things do remain about the time I met mother again. For one thing the house was suddenly clean; I no longer had to wade through piles of empty Halloween candy and apple wrappers. And the stink of my body that had kept all the kids at school even farther away from me than usual was gone. My hand was carefully cleaned where the blade had bitten me, my clothes were taken off and shoved in the garbage pail, my wet footprints were on my table again; I was naked and clean and running around again on black feet, and I was so happy I got the hiccups. For some weeks after, I hiccuped through life, getting happier each day. Mother would wake me in the morning and carry me to the yellow room where the tub was waiting, hot and stormy, and with my soggy bear floating in the middle and staring at me with eyes I had long since pulled out that said—but hasn't it always been like this?

Yes, I would think while being sunk like a rock. Yes, I would think while splashing around and drowning that eyeless bear again and again. And once, while thinking of nothing but yeses, I forgot who I was and peed in the water, I don't know why, and I watched in horror as the yellow floated to the top, erupting there in tiny bubbles of shame. But mother didn't hit, didn't shout, didn't even grow wrinkles; instead she kneeled down with her hands on the rounded edges of my tub, and she sucked at my water like a fish, blowing even more bubbles, and I got the hiccups again. When she heard me hiccuping all over the place, she rose up from the water and looked at me in the way one would look at a sea monster that wasn't supposed to be there. And then, and for the first time since I could remember, she laughed.

That laugh, and all its relatives, lived in our friendly apartment for many weeks. When I woke in the morning from a dreamless sleep she would be sitting on the edge of my army cot laughing. And whenever I asked her if she ever wanted me to go back to school again the whole of her large body would shake with laughter. At lunchtime and suppertime she would laugh over the stove that I had never seen used before, and whether or not she knew I was listening, and as soon as I was served she would stand way back to avoid getting hit by the violent storm my hands made of the food, and we would laugh together, she with her hands in the air for protection, and me with a full mouth and a naked face and body that must have looked like the insides of a garbage pail. Then, of course, and as soon as I had licked up the last of the gravy, there would be another bath, and another scrubbing with an old dog brush I had once found lying lonely in the schoolyard, and another hard toweling on the black table. And when I was done I think I probably looked as though I had been lying in the sun for a long time.

But one day, and for no reason I can remember, the sun went down and the laughter stopped, and I was back in school and back on my ration of sugar and raisins. And the visitors came back too, as though their vacations were over. I wasn't sent down to get them anymore, or their bottles in brown paper either, but except for that everything was normal again and my hiccups went away.

It was about this time that the first of father's many postcards began coming and I learned from them that for the past several years he had been a First Mate on a passenger ship that rarely came into an American port. In each of the ports he was now stopping at, he took the time to pick out a nice postcard for me, which he put into an envelope along with a coin of that country and a small paper flag from his ship, a red and white one on a gold pin that had the words Grace Lines printed on the white part. From the very first, I saved everything, the envelopes with the funny foreign stamps, the coins, the flags, the postcards with the pictures of camels, or ships blowing clouds of water into the air, or little brown boys no bigger than me wearing long striped coats and with their hands deep into the backs of fat white animals that I think now were probably sheep. I had all these treasures piled neatly in the closet of my room, next to my comic books and my Sunday shoes, which were only worn when the cheap ones fell apart. There was never any writing on the postcards, except for a small space in one corner that explained in sometimes two or three languages the pictures on the front. But this never mattered because it never occurred to me that any other writing was allowed; and I guess I probably thought father would surely be coming home soon and he would want to tell me all his wonderful stories in person. After a few months, my stack of postcards became so high I had to make two of them.

There was one visitor I remember better than any of the others. He was a tall quiet man with a black mustache and when I first saw him, I thought father had come back. I ran out of my closet and rushed up to him so fast I bumped into his legs, but when he jumped away as if I were a dog that might get hair all over his clothes, I knew that in spite of the piles of postcards, there really was no father, or if there was, he had no son.

But anyway, maybe because I had bumped him, he always treated me much nicer than the others did, not even laughing at the hairless dog that stared at him quietly all the time he was there. He came up many times, he was the only one in my memory to ever be invited back more than once, maybe because he was so nice to me. He brought me a deck of playing cards once as a present and showed me how to play solitaire on the black table. He taught me how to cheat, my first lesson in staying alive, how to pretend that if the card in my hand wasn't the one I wanted, it could really be the right one if I needed it badly enough and if I could put it down quickly, forcing it with all my might sometimes, not looking at it again, not even after I had won. Even though he seldom spoke to either mother or me, we became good friends. When I came home from school, he would be sitting at the black table with our solitaire cards spread out, and as soon as I came through the kitchen door he would stop his own game and begin again to try to teach me how many games there were to be played alone.

There were hundreds of solitaire games to be played, though at the time I only learned one well enough to play it when the man wasn't there. Years later, somewhere in my twenties, there would be a jail in New Jersey filled with silver bars and black men who had nothing in their hands except drug sores and time and the playing cards we made with my help from the pages of the library books that we weren't allowed to keep long enough to read. I turned myself into a card factory in that and in various other New Jersey, New York, Maryland, and Florida jails, children's homes, reformatories, and mental institutions, working against time to turn out deck after ripped-out deck for the worst of the bored to play whist with and poker and gin and knuckles and other games I now forget the names of that we all had learned well in other places. But when it came to solitaire, I was king, and those blacks along with the few whites were like little children; they knew about as many games of solitaire as I had known at the age of seven. So I taught them the many I had learned over the years and in return they crumpled up some of those library book pages into kings and queens and rooks and knights and bishops and pawns and taught me how to play chess and how to play time and how to fight with my hands and feet and how not to hate too much, only enough to get free again. And like that man with the black mustache who never spoke, not even to the silent guard of my mother who sometimes watched without ever understanding, we sat for long hours at tables, thick green metal ones, teaching and learning from children that there were and still are many games to be played even when one is so alone that the world might as well be gone.

But at the age of seven I already knew of some of the games one could play with cards when alone. Even before I was given the solitaire cards, I was already playing many games with the postcards father sent. And when I wasn't at school, or being bathed, or running around trying to figure things out, or sitting with the man with the mustache, I would think of what I had seen in mother's bedroom and I would take the black blunt scissors I had stolen from school and cut out parts of my comics, Superman and Superwoman and Elasticman mostly, and I would paste with flour and water their words and pictures on the empty spaces of the postcards just under the foreign languages. Sometimes I would get real excited, though I never made a noise, and while pressing the bodies of two Superheroes together I would make the little sounds in my mind that I remembered having heard when the ghosts were quiet. But one day, while mother was entertaining my friend with the mustache, my house of cards collapsed when I made the mistake of allowing my mind to open up just enough to let some of those sounds slip out. It was after a bath, and I was naked and sitting in the dust of my closet. My pasted postcards were flying around in the air over my head and talking to each other and getting very familiar. Then the first friend of my life walked in wrapped in a sheet and as quick as a game is lost he wasn't my friend anymore. When he saw my erection as straight as a finger he laughed, and as I sat there stumbling all over my tongue he did what so many would do in my future: he found my weak spot of the moment and stabbed. He kicked at the postcards and comics and at the rows of flags that were stuck in the floor, and he picked me up and carried me into the bedroom, I guess to show mother what a man I'd become. She too was wearing a sheet like a ghost, and drinking from a bottle that was wrapped in her hair. He dropped me on top of her, and that bottle that she pulled free of her hair in anger and then threw, exploded on his face. Then there was screaming, and when I opened my eyes I heard above the screams the slamming of a door, and except for the broken glass and a sheet all crumpled up and empty, there was nothing else on the floor, and I knew that the ghost of my first friend and only enemy had turned to ashes as surely as if he had touched a forbidden white string hanging above a tub.

2

In remembering that now, when the bitter and the sweet of hunger and of raisins were all wrapped up in a sheet when it was my turn to visit, to enter into the hole of the lion, I also think about that darker time when the moaning was done and the moaner was knocking at the door of my ear, asking me not in the voice of a lion but in the voice of a mouse if it was all right to come out. But when mother came out, my memory went out with her, like a light, making me forget whatever it was I wanted to at the time. Now why in the world would I mostly forget a moment that surely must have been a happy one, yet at the same time remember so well something I would just as soon forget?

Perhaps the dark spaces in my mind are there not only to keep memories in sane order, but also to play tricks so as to scare me away from reaching back too far or examining too closely the monsters that might be found there if ever by chance I should go beyond the light of order and sanity, beyond where life had intended.

I am not courageous. Boys in my past have knocked me down and stood over me to tell me this. But I remember them, sometimes even fighting against any dark spaces that might want to make me forget. And the eyes of teachers have swum over seas of raised hands only to sink in the empty space at the edge of the world where my hand alone was without the courage to rise at the chance of answering some silly question. But I remember them. Doctors also have remarked on my courage upon seeing two eyes flushing like toilets all over their clean dry inkblots. But with difficulty I remember them. And ten trillion dentists have stood in front of my mouth, each with the look of absolute amazement after having made the startling discovery that for the first time in all their tearless years of grinding holes in the faces of children, here was one that was wet. But I remember them. And when I was ten years old, and knew for certain what madness was like, I remember that too. And I remember also all the bars and the locks, and the long winding stairs to all the cells, and many of the faces of the men and the children that were in them; even though some are free now, they are still imprisoned in the cells of my mind.

I can easily remember most of all those things, even though I am as far from being courageous now as the child in my past was from being what the entire world expected. And like that child with my name who still giggles and cries and sits quietly in the semi-darkness of my memory, I am not afraid of reaching back to him any more than he was with his arm that time when he rammed it into the black hole of the old tree at the end of the playground of my second grade. So why can't I remember what happened after mother came out?

I will admit I have no courage, that the shadow of every moving and unmoving thing still scares me greatly if I come on it too quickly, but not that I am afraid to speak to the shadows within me. And even if my thoughts should rub against more than the webs of small spiders and wake up and be attacked by some monster of my memory or my imagination and come out a bloody chewed-off mess, I think I would probably shove that stump in again and beat that thing in my mind senseless until it changed into a chipmunk or something, the small and harmless form it should have taken the day it began its growing. So why can't I remember?

But perhaps that moment when mother came out means nothing after all, and the only reason I forgot it was because it was as dull as tying a shoelace, and I certainly can't remember all the times I did that in my life. Maybe she looked down and saw me standing dirty and quiet and thought for a second it might be better for everyone if she returned to the dark smelly room in back of her, but then took pity, saying—take off your clothes, they stink, start filling the tub, why haven't you washed yet, supper will be ready as soon as you're done. Yes, maybe that was the way it was. But then again maybe not. Perhaps the door crashed open and she was a wild thing without manners, screeching and crawling and eating the shit from the back of her dress that I vaguely remember smelling from where it had collected hard like glue during all those days of moaning. But again, and with a third and I hope more remote possibility, perhaps the wild thing was me, the shit was mine, the one who had attacked with a throat jammed with hate was indeed the very prosecutor, the memory expert, the littlest one there.

It was not too long after the slamming of the door by the man with the mustache that the door to our apartment was shut for good. It was in the middle of the second grade that the boredom had set in so deep there was no longer any room for me. I had an uncle in Boston who drove a Greyhound bus. Mother packed me up as quick as a heartbeat and took me on that bus, and it was a beautiful ride. She didn't talk to me on the long trip but I didn't mind because she usually didn't have much to say to me anyway. The funny thing was she didn't talk to the driver either. We were the only passengers and it would take many miles before I would find out the driver was the very uncle to whose house I was being delivered. After that I quickly learned that all my family hated each other, and each with good reason. And it didn't take too much time to learn that all of man belongs to that same family.

There was only one horrible moment during that lovely tree-swishing-by ride; because it took so long and because there was nobody on that empty bus to mention my problem to, I peed in my pants. Later on, when I was ten and riding on a train, it would happen again, and again everything under me would become wet, and again the feeling of guilt and of doom would seep upward like a poison and make me almost blind. But both times, the second ride also being a long and forgiving one, the person sitting next to me and beginning to feel her own bottom getting damp, would say—don't cry, don't worry about it, it's been a long trip and it could happen to anybody. This they both said, or something like that, but in the case of mother it was almost more of a shock to hear the unhappy voice filled with love than it was to find myself suddenly sitting in a puddle. And some months after that second ride, I would be playing in a half-built house with a girlfriend named Janet and I would notice then, and many other times too, that the crotch of her dungarees was dark blue and soaking wet. And unlike anything I would ever do, she would smile at me and giggle and sometimes even give a couple of wipes with her hand. And I would stare at her as if she were crazy, but be very kind about it, and very forgiving even though we hadn't been on a long trip at all. But at the same time I would want to shout—don't you see what you've just done, can't you understand that's a dirty disgusting thing to do? But I wouldn't say anything and she would giggle and wipe and we would go back to climbing the rafters or stealing the nails or writing our names in sawdust as if a world-shaking event hadn't occurred after all.

Anyway, after that wet Greyhound bus trip was done, I was taken into a white farmhouse by mother and the driver, and even before I could say where's the bathroom please, I was left standing with only half of the tour. I guess my mother probably said good-bye or something, I like to think she did. And right after my uncle had sadly introduced himself, his wife came out from somewhere and we all gathered around to hear the reading of mother's will. I had inherited nothing; uncle read the short good-bye letter she had written, and I cried for the first time in my memory.

Uncle's farmhouse was big and white. The fields all around were big too, cold and dead looking and wrapped in the sheet of that winter's snow. The only things that lived anywhere were the black branches in the surrounding woods that rubbed each other in the wind to keep warm, and the little brown mice that floated over the snow. I would chase those mice real slow like a friendly cat, but whenever they saw me too close they would misunderstand and go floating quickly home behind long white trails that would fall into dark holes. Then I would plop down in my snowsuit and wait for a very long time. But of course they never did come out again, they didn't even know my name, and sometimes I would get close and put my mouth to the holes to whisper my name again and again far into the earth.

But that never worked either and after a while I would forget about the life beneath and walk around the fields while waiting for the door of the farmhouse to open. Each day that door only opened twice, once to let me out after lunch and again to let me in as soon as the world got dark, so I would often lie down in the fields while waiting and think about mother, and wonder why it was I never went to school any-more, and why it was that none of my thoughts ever made any sense. I would watch the many cars rushing by on the road several big fields away, and I would take those people-filled cars in my eyesight between two fingers and slowly crush them like ants, pretending first to feel the warmness of the blood as it trickled like bathwater, and then the stickiness my hand still remembered from that time after it had grabbed the blade in the apple. And whenever I would again realize there was nothing I could do to hurt anybody else, or whenever my fingers became too tired, I would pretend to be a smudge of dirt blown to the snow by the wind and lie flat on my back with my arms and legs open as wide as my tight snowsuit would allow and pretend that all the people in the cars were talking about me, about the dirt that was ruining the clean snow several big fields away. And I remember too that many times more than once, when the road was empty of the people talking in my mind, I would unzip the front of my snowsuit and struggle to find somewhere beneath all those layers of clothes my soft friend that was always there, so as to prick him deep into the shock of the cold snow, as if trying to reach something, as if even without people liking me I could still be a part of the snow and the world, as if all nature, man mice and God, could know me so easily, know that already, at the age of seven and a half or so, I do somehow know that I am going mad.

After a time the door would open, and I would run at the signal and go into the house and be warm again and among people. I would take off my snowsuit and bask in the heat of the kitchen, filling my head with the many different food smells I had never known before, beyond that short time when the moans of mother had been replaced by her laughter over the stove, and while waiting for supper I would promise myself again to use only the best of manners.

All our meals always began and ended the same way. First, and in a low and patient voice while aunt sat watching in approval, uncle would explain to me the important differences between the main fork and the salad fork, the soup spoon and the jello spoon, and how there must be a slow neatness about eating, and above all that the meal should be totally without noises. Then I would nod and they would eat. My aunt and my uncle, their backs as straight as birds on a wire, would carefully and correctly and without a noise stab daintily at their pieces of meat and then lift them like moths to their mouths, chewing slowly, dabbing at their beaks with napkins to hide any knowledge of blood, moving their lips ever so softly as if upon wings. Then they would look at me, swallowing in my direction, caressing their water glasses with all but their little fingers, which were raised in the air like tails, waiting. And I would try, I swear I would try, but with every bite I took everything went wrong, the food on my fork or my spoon would fall all over the place, and the noises my mouth made were deafening. Then they would begin their shouting that would last for a long time, and their pounding on our table so hard I would shake, but all at the same time they would be laughing like birds who know they can kill without leaving their wire, and my throat would close, not opening again until the clearing and the leaving of the table, when the angry silence came.

Then, and after almost every supper, a different game was played. That aunt and that uncle had one thing only in common with mother; they liked the way my seven and a half year old body was put together. Later on in life I would be physically sick all the time and from every ailment that was ever invented, but never then. But they would pretend I was anyway. They were enema happy; they would stand smiling above my white tub that was soon to become dirty like the snow and enjoy the small body that was stuck onto a brown rubber tube as much as they would one of the butterflies at the end of a pin on the cardboard wall uncle kept in his study as a reminder he was bigger than most other things. I was afraid of that wall, and of the warm water that was so different from the snow, and I remember I pretended they were going to kill me, and it was a much better game than looking into the dark holes of mice.

3

One day they too packed me up for some reason of their own and I was driven from their house back to Connecticut and to another town to live with another aunt and uncle. I don't remember if I ever knew how any of these people were related to me, but I think perhaps the first uncle was mother's brother and the second aunt was mother's sister because, just like mother when I knew her, both were big and quiet and as different from me as loneliness is from a house full of people. These next members of my family were different also from my previous owners in that as soon as I was in their house, they promptly forgot I was there; they never took the time out to give me enemas or anything; they wouldn't look at me but through me, as if I were a pane of glass that must someday be put on a window ledge whenever they found the time or could afford the putty.

But I guess they were all too busy with themselves to be bothered with any of the problems a stranger might have. And they had a lot to be busy about. That house was a strange one. As soon as my first uncle had knocked on its door so my second uncle could start serving his time with me, he quickly turned and went back to his car not even saying good-bye, it's been nice having you with us, remember your table manners, or anything. And even before the door opened, I was already sniffing the strangeness that would be inside and all around me the second I stepped in. Except for the bathroom, there were dolls in every room of that house in which I was to live for almost three years, hundreds of them of every size, and each dressed differently, some with white ruffles starched as hard as coral, or with soft red silk and black stripes, or with pieces of animal skin both with and without hair, and all of them with human eyes that stared at me wherever I went. They were behind the open doors of tall glass cupboards, sitting quietly on tables and dressers and stools and chairs, surrounding the kitchen sink like kittens waiting to play with the tap of the water, heaped neatly in all the closets, piled legs over soft shoulders on the many long shelves of each room, and even sleeping with button eyes open on every well-made bed including mine. But the strangest thing, that which I would never really get used to, was their one and very important reason for being. The dress or costume or animal pelt of each was kept covered daily with the invisible wet contents of the dozens of perfume bottles that I would find several days after my arrival while looking under the bathroom tub for a sock I forgot I was wearing. The job of the perfume, the one it worked hard at but failed, was to cover up the thick smell of shit that was everywhere. The walls and ceilings and rugs and furniture and plates and spoons and everything else too smelled like those from a dollhouse that some angry little girl had flung into the mouth of a toilet that hadn't been flushed in years.

On my first day my uncle, a dark thin man who never stopped frowning, took me in to introduce me to that angry little girl and it was in her bedroom that the smell was strongest. My aunt was sitting in her bed, propped up and surrounded by dolls, looking angry, as if I'd been expected. She was much bigger than mother, and with layers of bloated yellow fat that kept fighting through her nightgown to fall on every inch of the bed some doll wasn't squeezed into. Above her huge wrinkled head that was cut with a red gash for a mouth and stabbed with two holes where blue marbles were sunk, there was a winter white cloud of hair; and when she pulled me over by the arm to get a better look at her sudden son, I remembered that time I was hit in the face with a snowball, when the hard ball exploded in my mouth and eyes with the smell of fear. But, and perhaps because she understood, she let me back away quickly, waiting a few more days before showing me the soft ugly ball from where the smell came.

It was in this week I fell in love with my first girl. There was a cousin who shared that stinky life with aunt and uncle and me. Her name was Bobby, short for Roberta, and she was in high school at the time I think, and all legs and arms and very kind and with a face I still see in my dreams right after a nightmare has gone away. She was beautiful in the way people are when they are the only ones to ever say anything nice, and as soon as I got up the courage, I asked her to marry me and she said okay and that was the end of that. I would follow her around the house from doll to doll on her daily trips of pouring perfume on those needing it most. I remember that even though she seldom spoke to me either, she liked me a great deal because sometimes on our trips around the house I would pretend to be looking at something else and then turn around real quick to catch her staring at me like one of those dolls. And two different times, months apart, once when some big girl at school had beaten me up because of a misunderstanding about the constant smell of my clothes, and again when the aunt had called me but all I had done was stand there and tremble and cry,

Bobby came over and without a word knelt down and drew me close into a skinny body that had no perfume and no other smells either, and I remember from those and many other times too she was much more scared of things than I could ever be.

Bobby had another job besides pouring perfume and she was told to teach it to me so I could help her get it done faster so she would have more time to do homework. She showed me how to fill the white basin with hot soapy water, how to rip up old cloths and stack them neatly on each of the trays that also carried into the aunt her breakfast each morning and her supper each night after school. We would take the trays in and place them on aunt's gigantic lap and then stand by the bed to wait for her to finish. When she was done, either I or Bobby would push the dirty dishes to one side of the tray and dip the first cloth into the basin and unbutton away the top of aunt's night-gown and unsnap the blue clips from each side of the brown belt that hugged tight to the fat stomach aunt's swollen rubber bag of shit. We would carefully take away the bag and the belt, placing them on one of the dirty dishes so they could later be carried to the black stool in the kitchen and be washed. Then, and with rag after rag, we would gently clean the red wrinkled ball of her protruding intestine, and all around it, being careful to catch in our rags any sudden squirts that might be thrown up from the tiny hole in the middle.

—One of her guts exploded ten years ago, Bobby once ex-plained while showing me how to fold a cloth thin enough to wash into the deepest of the wrinkles.

—And even after three operations my bum still doesn't work, I think I remember my aunt saying as she pulled closer, as she always did, the top edges of her nightgown so we wouldn't see her naked.

And then, and at other times too, and with my hands covered with the insides of my aunt's body, with everything on my hands that people try hardest to hide from view, I remember I worked very hard at trying to imagine what those baggy breasts would look like if only I could see them just once.

I didn't mind my job too much after the first couple of times, I don't know why; but there was one time many months later when I too was touched by the horror my cousin always seemed to carry with her like schoolbooks. It was after school one day that a great sound rumbled out of the mouth of the aunt and the tiny hole in the gut opened and then spit in the air a thin brown stream that splashed on my cousin's white face.

—It must have been the prunes, I think I remember my aunt saying.

After that we were more careful, ducking back or to one side at the slightest hint of a sound or movement.

I was in the third grade now, my school was a brick monster, I was eating well for the first time in my life, I was growing up, beginning to question things. I worked so hard on my many questions that sometimes while walking, in school or in the house or somewhere between, I would suddenly feel my feet stop when the realization reached down to them that the rest of me had stopped breathing. That feeling, and the warring against it, was I guess the first of the thousands of battles I would lose with myself over the years. I would stand where my feet had stopped and listen to the silence where my heart had before been thumping away madly like footsteps and wait with clogged ears for mother to start moaning again. The heartbeat would come back of course, and so would my breathing, but they would do so on their own: I would have nothing to say on the matter. It was during these times that I discovered I had no real control over my body any more than I had over the body of anyone else. I found out then my enemies not only surrounded me, they were inside too. And not just in my head, where the presence of an enemy had been suspected some time ago; but in my strong body also, the one turning red under mother's towel, the one being flushed with warm water in the butterfly collector's white tub, the one that could run faster than most other kids and jump up more stairs with fewer leaps than even any of the teachers probably could. This sudden knowledge hit me hard. It told me quite plainly in the way of a bored teacher drumming in geography that I was a stranger in my own body and not even a particularly wanted one at that.

It was spring when this happened. I remember it was spring because there were lots of little things in the air. There were bugs that had green windows for wings, round red seeds that fell slowly from trees, pollen that shot up from the grasses and the weeds, and other dusty bits and pieces, each and every one of which smashed at my nose and eyes each time I left the house. I would walk to school with my body going one way and my mind going off in a totally different direction, as if they hadn't known each other for eight years at all, and my hands would want to tear out the dirty roots of my itching eyes or at least dig open that closed hole of my throat. I would walk to school fighting for breath with every step, I would sit in the school chair with my hands clawing at the desk and my head held as high as possible and my mouth wide open, and my angry lungs would take over my body, tight inside me and trembling like fists. And it would be the same on the way home.

One day I frightened everybody by standing in the middle of aunt's bedroom and gasping for air and changing colors like a chameleon. Suddenly I was noticed, and somebody, I think it was Bobby, brightly suggested that perhaps I needed a doctor.

My hands were washed; the doctor came, said I had asthma, said, as many others would say over the years, that I would soon outgrow it, stuck two needles in my bottom, and when I awoke it was as bad as ever and I was forgotten again. But the kids in my third grade class didn't forget. They thought it funny that one of the fishes should always be sitting with his head out of the water. My house became a place to run to each lunch-time and evening at the airless bottom of an ocean with a school of loud sharks following. And even when I was safely inside, my lungs begging the rest of me, filling again and again with nothing but shit, those stupid third graders would stand outside making fish sounds with their healthy mouths and howling for me to come outside to be beat up, until finally either Bobby would yell at them, or the stink from the house, which was always powerful on hot days, would become too much and wash them away. I never did come out to be beat up; I think now it would have been better if I had; I think now an act of courage then would have gotten me breath, might have prevented all the years of cowardice to follow.

But I did try it just once, sort of as an experiment. It was because of a girl of course. Her name was Ann and I was holding hands with her in the line from the school to the sidewalk. There was a big bully in back of us who wanted to change places. To my great surprise I breathed in deep and said no and he hit me and I knocked him down. I'll never forget how powerful I felt at that moment. My lungs were clean and fat with air. All my mother's visitors lay at my feet. All my failing grades were passed. David had done in Goliath. I then walked Ann home, and after she had closed her door, I began my walk across a high grass field to my own house. Halfway down the path I looked up to see my Goliath waiting at the end of the field that was closest to my house with the whole Philistine army. My first thought on seeing six people hating was to run away. But how could I? It would be many years before I would finally be terrified enough to find the courage to run in a direction away from home. So I continued my walking, sucking at the heavy air, and I delivered myself into their pounding arms, never once saying a word or giving resistance. They beat me in the weeds for a long time, but all I did was fight for breath. When they were done, I went home.

That too was another defeat, not to my mind but to my body. In spite of that and other beatings to follow, I was able to keep some control over the mind I knew was sick. But each time my body got hurt for whatever reason, in that third grade and in most of my grades to come, it would seem so senseless and especially sad to me, not only because my body was the biggest thing about me but because, since everybody up to now had loved it so much, I had naturally become quite fond of it myself.

The breathing was always the worst thing. Much worse than anything else. In that third grade, and again in the sixth and seventh I think, and several times more as a teenager gone completely mad, my body was like a breathing machine somebody had forgotten to turn on full power. To have no control over the body is more frightening than anything the mind can do, or even anything that other more healthy minds can do to someone who is helpless, and not to be able to breathe is much worse than whole cellblocks of screaming madmen. That sixth grader in my future would peel the paint from the bars of his asylum cell, not out of craziness, though that was there too, but to keep his mind on breath, and also to cover the ugly birthmark on his neck with spit and flecks of green paint. That seventh grader, I think it was then, would fall one day on a hard sidewalk made of complete stupidity and break his stupid nose and not be so good-looking anymore, but worry only about how it would affect his breathing. And that teenager, in a nine-dollar-a-week wet basement room in New Jersey, furnished mostly with madness, would watch his teeth fall to the rotting wood of the floor and then crumble in his fingers when he tried to pick them up, but think only of breath and how to get more. But the strangest thing about all those times that the body got hurt was that it wasn't mine, it was always a sixth or seventh grader's, or that of a teenager I didn't know well enough to be able to help. And it was strange too how we fought back, mostly with me just looking on, wishing and hoping and looking silly. With every beating there was a search for another, even though the searcher was such a coward it had to be done unconsciously, and even though it was discovered, because of a toughening of spirit or something, that winning was in fact quite possible once in a while. For instance, every time a tooth fell out or was knocked out or pulled out, there was a wide smile at everything for days. Or, and when deepest in need of breath and at every chance, kittens and flowers and weeds and even fingers of dirt were picked up and breathed in deep so that the choking smell of the hair or the pollen or the earth could challenge the pain, could put up a good fight to punish it and hurt the hurting.

As in most of the houses of my childhood and after, there was in that third grade a garden in back of the house and a woods beyond. Most evenings, after I had helped Bobby clean aunt as neat and as white as I had once cleaned ants from sugar, and after we had all eaten, I would go into the garden and play there or walk or just sit, swatting at the bugs, studying everything, doing my best to fill my insides with the sweet air, praying, even though I still didn't yet pray, that soon the air would be a little nicer. I would walk or sit or draw my name in the dirt and grass and put green things to my mouth and begin

---

sweating and sneezing so much that after a while Bobby would hear me and come out to bring me back in. Once inside I usually felt much better, and in spite of the dripping from everywhere of the smell of the shit, my breath would return, my eyes and body would dry up and stop itching, and I would pretend that the eyes in my slowly unclogging head were as blue and as normal as any of those from where the hundreds of dolls sat laughing.

But that is enough of that. I don't want to think of it any-more. I want to think of other things. I want to remember the good things that lived in that garden and house. It has always been an iris garden in my thoughts, filled with yellow and purple and white flowers that continue to wave in the wind of my memory as if they still think it necessary to apologize for all the discomfort they once caused. I never saw them growing and I never saw them dying, though I suppose they probably did both. I only remember them planted there like good things in a memory.

There was a red iris too, a friend of mine, a great big bloody thing taller than the others and with a feathery top so heavy it looked down on all the others as if trying to figure out just why it should be so different. And once, while I was busy watching a beetle go to the bathroom on a brown bud, I saw in one eye's corner the most magnificent sight: I saw that red iris say to hell with all this and then explode in a flash of sun-lit wings and disappear way up and beyond where my wet eyes could see.

But of course there was an explanation. Isn't there always? I caught my breath and ran into the house and told Bobby exactly what I had seen. But instead of getting excited, she got a bird book and opened it to the page on Scarlet Tanagers. Oh well. It was still a miracle. Sort of.

But there were other miracles in back of that house that not even Bobby could have explained if ever I had asked her opinion, which I didn't. Beyond the garden and deep in the woods there were dark places under pine trees that smelled better than flowers and where one could pretend to be lost. And holes in the earth between roots where rabbits lived. And above them friendly branches where one could climb very high and wait for a while, swaying in the wind, spitting down white drops on the world. And the rain dropped pine needles to be sucked at with the very tip of the tongue. Snapping turtles that musn't be touched. Sun falling gold into green and dark purple. An owl hooting close from a trillion miles away. A bright black pond where frogs jumped when I came near. And the soft crashings of birds through branches when the real or false monsters of their imaginations too took flight beyond all moments of stopping to think. And it was there on a branch that I thought, that I began to think for really the first time. Even as my eyes saw deeper into the dark woods, my mind too expanded. I could feel it. I remember I could feel it. There was without a sound an opening of eyes and ears, a seeing and a listening and a light that lit up my entire skull like a jack-o-lantern, or so it seemed, and I stayed on that branch for a long time, drinking in the feeling, getting so drunk that later on, when the woods had become nightmare dark, I found myself laughing all the way to the house and so loud that no other sound could possibly have existed without first asking me.

There were many good miracles in the house also. My cousin was every one of them. After the cleaning of the aunt and the eating of the supper and the thinking and the sneezing in the woods and garden, Bobby would lay her high school homework on a table and I would sit in a chair nearby to watch. The arithmetic and other things weren't much fun and she would complain often, not in words of course because that might disturb aunt, but with lips and eyebrows and with her short brown hair shaking on both sides of her tense face each time there was a problem I couldn't even begin to help her with. But those things were done with fast, and as soon as the table was cleared of books and crumpled paper and broken pencils, the large shiny posters of her art class would be taken from a closet guarded by dolls, and spread on every inch of the table. Thick plastic rulers of all colors including the see-through elbow kind would be pulled from her schoolbag. Then would come the thin paint brushes and the fat drawing pencils, which were placed in neat rows on the posters, with a yellow sharpening box in front like a general of an army. Then the best thing, the little jars of paint from where the real magic would march. And her face, and mine too I guess, would stop looking dead just as the posters would when the whites of them retreated on both sides of the rulers so that every color in the world, or at least in the jars, could be brushed on with a concentration and even a kind of madness the happy like of which I have never seen since.

I don't remember what any of those assignments were about, perhaps she invented them in order not to be sad all the time. I think that was the reason because I know none of my teachers ever gave me any posters or paints, all they ever gave me were dirty looks whenever my breathing got too loud. But I remember well the lines on my cousin's posters that crossed each other making big and little boxes, each one perfect, each one of a different pastel color. I don't know if the reason for them was invented or not, or if it matters much either way, but I do know we shared an excitement for color that would stay with me for years, shining especially bright during the ones that were darkest.

In one of my future jails, for instance, I would be allowed to organize an art class for the black and white men, using yellow soap and also the brown shoe polish which was sometimes drunk, and boiling their old socks into dyes of more colors than they had ever seen before. And in the fifth grade, I think it was the fifth, there would be a contest given by the Poppy People on Poppy Day to see who in our school could make the best posters memorializing our men that the war at that time was killing. I don't remember what the first and second prizes were, or even really what war they were being awarded for, but I know the third was seventy-five cents because when it came in the mail, I immediately spent the check on candy and then was sorry because I had no proof that I had won. I also remember thinking that it wasn't very fair for us young kids to be competing against the older classes, but then perhaps my memory is playing tricks because some of those kids were pretty old and surely the Poppy People wouldn't have wanted us to fight against men. But anyway, and thanks to the memory of my cousin, I won my first and last prize and boy was I proud. I hadn't been that proud of myself since a day some weeks before when some ugly girl had asked me to a movie I had already seen. And after spending my seventy-five cent prize on teeth-killers, I begged more money from somebody and bought more candy and then got to thinking I could do it again, and begged money a second time to buy some posters and a tin of water paints. But except for some of my paintings in that art class of that future jail, none of my works ever came to much, perhaps because no prizes were ever offered, beyond an escape from boredom. But in my fifth grade, two years away from Bobby and five before the first jail, there were prizes still to be offered. I remember that the best of the school posters were displayed in the store windows of our small town. All along and on each side of the main street almost every window was taped with some kid's poster. Mine was in a butcher shop right under a neon sign that kept flashing on and off in the color of blood— Fresh meat for sale here. There were many white crosses on my poster and some words I no longer remember that I had stenciled on a green grass background. And in one top corner, as in one top corner of all the window posters, there was a red paper poppy pinned by a black ribbon that had on it a soldier's name and the letters, Pfc., which I thought at the time meant Poster finished correctly.

Forgetting now about my future art and jails and wars, I remember my cousin had other ways to keep us from being sad. Sometimes at night, when uncle as usual was working late in the gas station that I think he owned, and when aunt was snoring louder than the crackling of french fries, I would watch Bobby cut those potatoes into thin slices and then dip them into hot deep fat until they turned brown and crisp and strong enough in smell to chase away the stink of the sleeping aunt and make eating possible. This was Bobby's best thing, and for hours, or so it seems now, we would crunch away in the darkness while smiling at each other, while pretending that things were different somehow.

Bobby was kind of strange in her own way. I remember one evening when she hopped all smiles into the smelly living room, knocking some perfumed dolls off a shelf in her rush to show uncle and me the very first dress she had ever worn. Uncle turned a page in his paper and without looking up asked how did it feel, and that proud girl, only half as proud as I was for her, flopped her hands like dead fishes behind her and in front of her and to both sides, and then said—but there's no pockets, what do I do with my hands if there's no pockets to hide them?

And once, some months later and late at night, while I was

busy chewing during one of our french fry feasts, she knelt
before me in the darkness and struggled with those dead fishes
to unzip a fly that was just as stuck in time as we were. She
pulled and pulled at my rusted zipper and then got up and took
my empty plate to the kitchen.

There was another miracle at the end of that third grade.
Several houses away there was a lady so sad and lonely that
sometimes her loud talk and soft screamings would leave her
wood porch in the blackest of our neighborhood's night and
turn on the eyes of other houses that would shine in questions
asking—how dare you, how dare you be crazy and wake us?
Then I, like other kids and owners of kids, would open a
window and listen between panes to a lady as crazy as a cock-
roach shouting to the world that the world was not quite what
it should be. Once in a while, whenever someone complained,
a cop car would come by to tell her to be quiet and I would wait
for a while, watching the red light flashing in front of the crazy-
house, and then go back to bed knowing she would only start
again once the light had gone. I think about this now and I
realize there were really two miracles about that lady. The first
miracle was that she was the only one.

But it was the second that was the best. One day, and I
don't remember this ever happening again with anybody, that
lady forgot her loneliness and gathered up every kid in the
neighborhood. It was after school and when I came by, I saw
three or four kids from my school standing on her lawn waiting

patiently in the hope that the crazy lady on the porch would start yelling in the daytime for once. But instead of yelling, she just stood there bent over like a kid, with her skinny arms resting on the wooden rail, and with her eyes staring back over the glasses that hung on her nose. I joined the kids and waited with them, and then more kids came by, and soon there were about a dozen of us, all waiting in happy silence for the crazy lady to start yelling.

And when she thought her audience large enough, she left her porch and walked slowly down the steps to the soft grass in front of where we were all backing away and said—do any of you know the rules to Kick-the-Can?

Some among us did, and we played it that afternoon, and we played that and many other games on her lawn for many nights after. We played Red Light and Statues and Mother Goose and Hide-and-Seek and Giant Steps and Prisoner's Base and Nuts-in-May and Animals and Spud and Lightning and Colors and Doors and Red Rover with a ball bouncing up and over and down the sides of the crazy house; and each of these games and others were played with that crazy lady reminding or informing us of the rules, making sure the two sides were always even, laughing no matter which side or which kid won, and sometimes letting the little kids win just to hear the sounds of their laughter, and running to help whenever someone fell down on a rock or was pushed into a tree.

It was in this month that I started to breathe again, that I was glad to be alive, that I stopped being lonely. It was also in this month that I felt the sadness some people feel when the best of their friends is taken away. Not all of us kids were there at that moment; some had become bored with such organized games. But those of us who were left standing on the far side of the street were hurt real bad, even if only for a few days, by the incredible sight one evening of a cop car with a flashing red light that finally took away our crazy lady.

That summer was empty and, except for my turning nine and getting a bow and arrow set from Bobby, I remember nothing from it. The autumn that followed shares itself in my memory with most of the ones before and after, almost all of them a beginning of strange teachers and of things taught I could never understand, a deeper and crueler awareness all over again that I was different from those who were learning, an unholy number of autumns and fourth grades fused by the devil of my memory into an entire world set afire by the torch of a single gold tree held in the dirt-fist of a small-town corner. That tree, only one to each autumn and a different one each time, would shake the trillions of its tiny flames in the wind until they went out and got black and fell each year on my asthma breath that at first always came hard with the violent and final stirring of the pollen, and then soft and easy with the thankful breaking of the brittle embers I would smash to ashes in my fingers. Then winter comes as it always does, all of them too, pretty much the same, black bony trees ashamed for being naked and rubbing branches to keep warm, fat proud evergreens offering armfuls of snow, heavy clothes smelling of moth balls and soap and even heavier galoshes smelling of rubber and dirty water, with big silver buckles that weren't silver and would never stay buckled, cold black cats crying in the snow and not very dangerous dogs sniffing at yellow, and all with cold eyes and hair hung with ice and slipping and sliding or getting stuck; and cold looks from old eyes at undone homework, cold buckles and zippers and books and doorknobs and railings and ears and noses and toes and fingers all the way to the wrist, warm hallways and rooms and beds and soups and radiators, and the silver moon sunk under the silver ice and always in the very middle of a puddle that breaks to pieces when I jump.

All my memories of winter are like that, sharp pieces stuck together in my mind to form one, a white and black and quiet time as cold as death, a time without miracles except for the snowmen and the falling of the snow and the icicles hanging everywhere that could be broken by quick hands or snowballs or sticks and used as daggers to stab invisible enemies until they melted. And a time of the easy blowing of my breath into smoke or on ice or at candles.

That's all there was to winter, mostly. But there was a red sled once with silver runners as sharp as anything. And one year, somewhere in my memory, I got a brand new Schwinn bike that was also red and that had a silver tire pump taped to one side and a loud golden horn just above the light. Even without presents, Christmas week was always fun in a magical sort of way, the miracle of the birth of the Christ Child and all of that. But even when there was a large tree piled at the cotton bottom with presents for everyone, including me, all neatly tied with red and blue ribbons and gold name cards and all, all those things were always ripped or broken or stolen or lost right after they were found, or so it seems now, and together with the time and the feeling, they all seemed to melt much too quickly; the snow went at the same time as did the fear of the fast sled, the tires on the bike exploded during a quick charge down a hill, the silver tire pump with the black hose was either stolen or lost or drowned in a puddle, the batteries to the light gave out, the golden horn rusted and wasn't any fun anymore. And the laughter of Christmas was put away until next year; the strings of lights and the balls of colored glass and the heaps of cotton and the tree each year were all dragged out to the garbage and burned.

If there was one real miracle in the winter of my fourth grade, it was City Hall. I didn't know then what happened there, but I know now it was a place where people met to decide upon the sidewalks to be shoveled that week, and the sewers to be opened, and the crazy ladies to be taken away, and upon the various other questions that might mean life or death to a Democracy. I passed this massive granite building each day on my way to school and again when coming home. I think it was in the month of Christmas that I first decided to explore. I had just gotten a wooden train set and some iron soldiers and a tin of water paints from Bobby and some new clothes and a pogo stick that I'd always wanted from my aunt and uncle, and the magic of all these new things was still in my mind. Each day I became braver, going farther up the steps for a week, and then deeper into the halls each day for another. In my third week of discovering the insides of this building that was empty of people most of the time, I found one day the many echoing tunnels that seemed to run beneath it for miles. There for the first time in my life, except for my days in the summer woods, I felt totally alone, buried deep in the snowy earth far under any cities of sad children. I couldn't open any of the doors I found in the tunnel halls, but I pretended to, which is almost the same thing. For some reason I don't know, the tunnel formed a jail in my mind with the hundreds of the town's prisoners reaching out their arms from their bars, asking and begging me to give them comfort. And Lord, did I try to give them what they wanted; I ran shouting through those empty halls, I crept through them slowly while talking to the men, with my back rubbing close to the brick walls so the arms wouldn't grab me and maybe pull me in too, and I prayed in the halls, even though I still didn't yet pray, that here, Lord, is real pain and here also is a secret that nobody else knows about and please let it stay that way. And then of course in school I told everybody. I gathered both big and little kids around me in the school hallways and playground and I said proudly to all—guess what, there's a jail at the bottom of City Hall, yes, and there's ten and fifteen prisoners to each cell, yes, and they never get fed or washed or anything, no, and yes, they are all screaming and hungry and eating each other and shitting on the floor, and come on let's all hurry up and get there to see them before they all die for God's sake. . . .

And all those kids believed me too, even after I had taken them there and they had seen for themselves there wasn't anybody, not anybody to laugh at, not anybody to help, no one at all. And there were no apologies to be made for the absence of those dead and dying men, partly because we felt that the prisoners and their cells had been moved to some other and much deeper part of the building so as to keep them beyond the eyes of children, but mostly because we all had to believe, and beyond all the evidence to the contrary, that somewhere in this world adults too, and not just kids and crazy ladies, were screaming.

But as with everything else, there was one day an end to this game. I was caught talking too loudly in a school hallway by a teacher who then slapped me with a hand that was as hard as reality is whenever it hits an imagination not invented in school. I was pushed into a closet and slapped again along with some stupid kid I had taken on one of my many guided tours. And when that kid squealed, I was beaten all the way up the stairs to the high school classrooms, and I was made to wait in front of one while my cousin was called to take me home for the day as punishment. That was the end of our love affair. All the way to the house, and for a long time after, Bobby hated me because I had interrupted her art class.

4

It was on a hot and airless spring day, and toward the end of that fourth grade in which I would fail everything including art, that the front door of our house was suddenly opened on a beautiful painting. My father, whom I hadn't seen since the age of three or four, was beaming at me all smiles and love as was the woman standing beside him, who I would soon learn at the touch of a kiss was to become my new mother. I cannot remember a happier moment. All the mice had come to the top of the earth. David's slingshot was working again. The prick could be returned to the snowsuit. The enema tube could be pulled out. The glass was shattered.

My God, but she was beautiful. And by that oven of a woman, and in the doorway between the unbreathable heat of the outside and the terrible stink of the house, actually stood my father, real and alive and not in dreams or thoughts or on post-cards either, and with a black mustache as I remembered and a handsome head so high it touched the top of the doorframe, even when he ducked beneath it to come in to ask me if I wanted to live with them. But all I did was cry and make a fool of myself. The tears poured from me warm and quick, just like that time on the Greyhound bus, but from the top this time and not the bottom. And then they were in and the door was closed, and right after the woman said how cute I was for all of my crying and everything, my father asked me if I wanted to kiss my new mother-to-be, as if such a thing could possibly be in question. My God, when they bent down I kissed them both half to death; they had to tell me to be quiet and to go away and sit like some excited dog. I did sit, panting I think, swimming for a long time in the clean breathable air.

I cried a lot then, and in front of everyone. But except for a certain excitement, I remember that my tears were sort of phony in a way and I'm not really sure why. Three or so years before when real mother had left me with the first aunt and uncle, I had cried in the same way. It was not so much that I then knew, as I somehow did, that I would never see real mother again or, at my second and last crying of my life, that I was overwhelmed by anything more exciting than any normal dog would feel. I cried both times because it seemed the right thing to do, it seemed what the adults at the time wanted and expected. Crying seemed proper simply because there wasn't anything else to do at the moment. A few months later the new mother who had inherited me would tell me with a sad look on her face that my old father had just died of T.B. in a Merchant Marine hospital in San Francisco and I would put on the same kind of act, though keeping the tears inside. It was not that I didn't care. I did care. I knew father was a good man, and I knew that he was intelligent and loved life and so must have known for several weeks that he was going to die. And being a part of me, however distant, I felt I knew of some of the horrible fear he must have felt. But for me it was just another change in my life. It was just another someone either coming or going away. They say that his handsome face had turned yellow and shrunken toward the end, that it looked like a head nailed to the hut of a headhunter in a country where they do such things. It was because of the way he looked that his ten-year-old son was never brought to visit him. New mother wanted me to remember him as he used to be. I guess she must have meant his photographs, the ones where he still stands tall and proud in my memory, dressed in the clean white uniform with the gold braid and the red and blue ribbons. But anyway, I was never brought to see him, and nobody else was either, not even during those first hospital months when he was still handsome and healthy looking. It surely couldn't have been he who barred my visits. I knew he loved me, he told me once; I knew of course he wanted to see me, of course he wanted to see his own damn son. Didn't he?

But anyway, and not too many months before that death that both did and didn't matter, the door to aunt's house opened; I cried for the last time in my life; the door closed and then on that same day opened again so that father and new mother and I could leave that house of shit and go to another. Uncle couldn't say good-bye to me because he was at work; he would get his happy surprise later in the day. And aunt couldn't either; she was snoring in her bedroom and farting from her stomach, so loud that new mother jumped a little each time, trying even more at each jump not to breathe in the strange air or be caught staring at the hundreds of dolls that stared back. But cousin Bobby was there; she giggled at each fart and jump and told me at the door she had forgiven me for my interruption of her art class by kissing my mouth good-bye in a long wet kiss that covered every problem and made me fall in love with her all over again.

So off we went, with and without good-byes, and on a train this time, a long streamlined piece of steel out of New Haven, its wheels beneath me burning all along the two thousand and more miles of track toward new mother's house with a song that rumbled and creaked over and over and filled my head like pollen from a garden with the music—Idaho, Idaho, you're going to live in Idaho, Idaho, and never be unhappy again.

On the first day it was mostly the fenceposts and telephone poles that I watched from my window whenever I got tired of trying to hear what my father and new mother were talking about in low whispers and giggles in the seat in front of me. With one hand I would play with the handles of the suitcases sharing my seat, drumming them in time with the music of the wheels that no one else seemed to be hearing, and with the other I would count the posts and the poles, trying hard, as I would do on all future trips, to figure out the differences between some things and others. I couldn't understand why the ones in the distance should crawl by so slowly, when in the same window, the ones closer up zipped by so fast that the closest of them were gone even before they could be correctly counted. Years later, or perhaps it was months or days, somebody would give a name to it, telling me I had discovered perspective. But I remember I still wouldn't understand, and that the attaching of a name to a problem couldn't solve that problem at all.

At the end of the first day our train stopped at Chicago so we could get off and get sandwiches and then run back quickly to a second train before it left without us. And again father and new mother sat in the seat in front, trusting me completely and without a word not to let anyone steal our bulging suitcases. Several times I peered over the back of their seat to see if their hands were still holding onto each other as if each was afraid the other might get up and run down the aisle never to be seen again if just for a second the touch was broken. I was glad they liked each other and I loved them both, but I couldn't see why it had to be me who was guarding the suitcases all the time. As much as I loved them, I thought that if someone had walked over to give me a knife, I would have stabbed it deep in either just to be able to sit holding hands with the other, even if only for a few miles. I would hold my hands tightly together for hours, wishing one of them would die, then be ashamed of such terrible wishes, then wish them all over again. But after a while I began to forget about the strangers who by now had long forgotten about me. I stared through my dirty window at the yellow fields that waved at me and my train for long miles until finally my counting of them put me to sleep where I counted them still and over and over with the help of the music of the wheels.

On my second and third days there was mostly desert in my window and little to count beyond an occasional water tower or grain silo that meant there might be a tiny town somewhere if I looked hard and quick enough. At one town that was there for a second and then gone, I felt a tap on my shoulder that sent a shock all the way down to my feet. It was the big foreign lady with the mustache who had been sitting across from me since Chicago with a little brown boy who hadn't once stopped chewing on the largest loaf of bread I had ever seen. In English as broken as her teeth she asked me if I wanted a sandwich and even though I didn't, I said yes. She gave me a loaf of bread as thick as a leg and so heavy with meat slices I almost dropped it. I thanked her and she asked me if I wanted to talk to her son, who was very lonely, and I nodded while trying to figure out what I would do with a sandwich that could have fed the entire train. The boy chewed and smiled and changed places with his mother and began talking to me in a voice so low that even if it hadn't been carried across our aisle by a foreign language I still wouldn't have understood a word. I chewed and smiled back. His mother nodded and smiled. Not knowing what to say, I didn't say anything, and after a few miles the boy stopped talking, his black marble eyes staring at me for miles over his lonely sandwich. I put mine in my lap. It was as useless as everything else.

After the desert there came mountains and then more desert. I got sick somewhere in the mountains, or maybe it was in the desert, and I threw up all over my window and couldn't see a thing through it. And when the foreign lady and new mother came over, I threw up again and again, on the suitcases and the sandwich and the helping hands holding handkerchiefs, and on just about everything else in my world. The mess poured from me like from a broken faucet and instead of the music, I heard terrible sounds. Then the bottom pipe burst and it poured from there too and with a smell so bad even aunt would have complained. But of course nobody did complain. That would come later. In a few days new mother would tell me I had ruined a trip that up to then had been real nice and peaceful.

There were two other things about that trip that I wouldn't really think about until long after the train had finally stopped. One was that father had coughed the whole time, though I wouldn't remember having heard that sound until a day a few months later when I learned both he and it were dead. Another was that I had discovered much more than just the perspective of close and far-away posts and poles; I had learned, without being aware of it then, what it was that could make a person mad.

It was not a physical thing that could do it, like asthma or a bad allergy or anything like that. My choking asthma was gone now anyway because of the difference in climate or something and wouldn't come back to hurt me until the climate changed again, and until sanity itself had gone and come back and gone away again. And my allergies to growing things had now turned over as tame as kittens and would only return, and in a mild way with wet eyes and small sneezes, when I actually picked one up to sniff deep in its fur.

No, it wasn't anything physical. And it wasn't the sudden loss of hope either, when the loneliness of the train had poured out from my top and bottom because of the feeling I had that of all the people on the train, I was the only one who wasn't going anywhere. I know it wasn't that because hope never really goes away, not even from the maddest of the mad. Sometime later, though how much later I don't remember, and while sitting with them on the floors and benches of my first insane asylum, I would learn all this again. I would learn that loneliness is one of the main causes of the disease, and that as long as there are people around somewhere, even if only on the other side of the bars or the peep hole in the door or half-dead on the same side, there is a hope the disease can be cured, even if only for a day or a lifetime or a second, if only a someone could take it into his head to talk about something, if only someone spoke. And while sitting and waiting quietly with them, thinking of these things, sharing their twisted thoughts and all they had, drinking from those same dented cups, cups with handles missing like heads without ears, I would listen, always listen, and even when there weren't enough words to go around, I would still find myself able to keep, as all the other inmates kept, one tiny place in my mind where I could go, as into the eye of a storm.

It would be several months later and while erasing the blackboard of my fifth grade that I would learn for the first time just how stupid I had always been by never really seeing my loneliness, by never even knowing it was there to be seen, not even once during all those especially bad times when it should have been obvious to me that my suffering or my strangeness, or both together, couldn't possibly have been caused by anything physical, or by anything at all that made any sense. I stood at the blackboard, breathing in the white dust of the words and numbers and pictures that were slowly vanishing in my hand, and I thought of the class behind me, quiet children sitting in hard chairs, and of all the days behind me, and of all the ones that were still to come, and I began to envy that brown boy on the train who at least had the fat woman with the broken teeth to talk to. Our teacher that day was telling my class of the wonders of communication and how advanced our century was in comparison with the pigeons, smoke signals, and pony-express riders that carried, smoked, and rode in other and less fortunate times. Telephones and telegraphs and telephotos and televisions were mentioned, including the joke about tell-a-woman, which made everyone laugh, and even another about telepathy, which didn't. It was when the teacher got into cars and trucks and buses that I looked out a window to see again the thousands of close and far-away fenceposts and telephone poles that were whizzing past my mind as fast as a train could go, and even though I had done a good job in making the blackboard as clean as a forgotten past, my fingernails got lonely and scared and left my mind and dropped the eraser and began screeching down the black slate so hard that some broke, making everyone in the silent class complain, making again the terrible sounds I had heard on the train.

I was sent right home after that of course, and with a note from the principal which I buried in the biggest ant hill I could find without even reading it first. I remember when I got home father was sitting in his usual chair in the corner and coughing up and spitting into a silver bucket his usual rusty balls of phlegm. I held up my hands to him, proud of the ten bandages the nice school nurse had rewarded me with. Later, I ripped them off, sucking at the bloody gauze, praying for God to kill him because all he had done was glance for a silent second at those magnificent bandages before continuing his coughing and his spitting. That prayer was the first of my life. Never again would I misuse such power.

The house my memory is now living in is owned and operated by the old mother and father of new mother. The reason we have come here is because we had no place else to go. Father had been fired from his ship because of the disease that same ship had given him in some foreign port, and real mother had disappeared, and there wasn't anybody else who wanted us. Father has come to this town to find a job so that someday soon we can all get married and have a home of our own.

—There's a nice one for sale at the edge of town by the desert, over on Spring Street, dark pink with blue shutters, not too far a walk from school, if only we could get the money, and a big lawn in back to play in and grow a garden maybe, I think I remember father once saying from his dark chair in the corner.

But there are not too many jobs in our desert town for a First Mate on a passenger ship, so mostly what he does, when he isn't out looking for jobs or houses for sale, is stay home and cough. He will be dead soon anyway, so what does it matter?

Our house of strangers where nothing mattered was an old gray house surrounded by lots of other old gray houses in an unfriendly neighborhood that sat quiet and smelling of death in the middle of a green oasis-like town in the middle of an empty desert valley that had once been a shining lake so many millions of years back that nobody I talked to could remember it. It was in this town that I would begin to grow up, begin to dream of lakes, grow to love all towns and deserts, and to hate all houses and people. I hated that house more than any of my others. It smelled forever of death, not only of mine and my father's, but of the dozens of dead bodies of the salmon and trout grandfather caught from the Snake River each Saturday and Sunday so grandmother could clean them each Monday and Tuesday so all of us could eat them each Wednesday, Thursday, and Friday. On weekends we usually had chicken.

Unlike grandfather, who only came home to sleep and eat and pick up his fishing tackle, grandmother never left the house. She was as much a part of the house as one of its wrinkled shingles, and as gray and dead-looking as the fish she was constantly cleaning and cooking. I don't remember too much about grandfather, except for the one time he beat me on the lawn with his fists because I had stolen one of his handmade fishing lures. It was orange and blue, the same colors as my school flag, and as soft as a cat, and to look at it you wouldn't think it had claws that could kill at the snap of a mouth. Grandmother was the same way, without the color and the softness, but small and with the ability to kill each time she opened her mouth in the direction of father or me, which was often.

I think perhaps it was new mother who disappointed me most in that house. I would forgive the kids and the teachers of my fifth grade, sort of, because I would know that their dislike of me was mostly my fault. And I forgave father because of his sickness, and besides, since I had never really known him before, perhaps he had always been that way, quiet and grumpy and all, speaking only to silver buckets. And since both grandmother and grandfather, as new mother told me to call them, had hated both me and father ever since the very first day, I had no more feeling toward them than the madmen in my future would have toward attendants. But I would never forgive the beautiful lady I had kissed in Connecticut. Sometimes I would pretend to, of course, thinking that maybe she would forgive me back for whatever I had done to her that was making her treat me with the same quiet contempt I got from everybody else whose lives I had somehow made less happy. Sometimes I would make believe it was really the other way, that I was really a nice normal kid new mothers and others couldn't help but like. Such pretending made me warm inside, made me smile and pretend even harder. Sometimes I would make believe that new mother was really cousin Bobby grown up, and that it wasn't either me or my father that was making her frown all over the house, and that at any minute she would begin to walk slowly around the house, pouring on dolls the perfume from tiny bottles to get rid of the fish smell. And as I used to do with Bobby, I would sometimes pretend to be watching something else, such as the wind in a curtain or a fish in a pan, and then turn suddenly to see if she was watching me. But unlike Bobby, she never was. And this game too one day ended when in the kitchen I turned too quickly and lost my balance on the slippery floor and fell with an arm smacking on the handle of a pan out of which then jumped in the air for the last time two silver trout.

There was one day with new mother that I remember better than all our others. It was School Registry Day and there was an agreement between us that I would be a big boy and go to the school alone and sign in for my fifth grade by myself. But it was a silent agreement, the kind people reach after weeks of not talking. It hung heavy between us and over our breakfast table, scaring me because I didn't want to do it alone, yet had no way to say so, making her smile over her coffee because she knew how afraid I was. We were alone that day, except for father who was coughing upstairs in the bathroom, and after she had left me to go to work in the town's only beauty parlor that she would later be able to buy with father's insurance money, I stayed at the table for a long time, just me and that agreement staring at each other in horror over a glass of milk and a bowl of soggy cornflakes and a torn-out milk-and-jelly-stained page from the town's newspaper that had on it in big black letters the instructions for all the school's children on where to go. I read every word of that page over and over as if looking for the instructions on courage, as if there might be some hidden sentence written especially for children like me that I'd overlooked before. I read the page so many times that even if I had found such a sentence, I wouldn't have understood it anyway because with each reading, the meaning of the whole page became more lost, the big black letters more blurred and senseless, the round wet marks made by my milk glass more confusing to read through, and the bloody thumbprints from my jelly sandwich more scattered and frightening. I had long before realized how alone people are, but it had never hit me so hard that even when a person is all alone, he still has to get up sometimes and do a difficult thing without anybody's help. There had always before been a hand to take me into a bad situation, or at least someone nearby to instruct me every inch of the way until I got out, but since this was the first time in my life I had ever been expected to go somewhere and do something all by myself, I decided that I must meet this, my first responsibility, square in the face, and I did so by crying tearlessly and also by walking. I walked so much back and forth between the safety of the table and the reality of the door that my legs began to ache, not only from the walk, but from the hard rubbing pressure of my fingers that wanted so much to send my legs to school while they themselves, as if cut off from reality, stayed home to play and to make perhaps another jelly sandwich. I walked and rubbed for hours, and when lunchtime came and new mother walked in, I was still somewhere between the table and the door, having decided for absolutely the last time that this time I was finally going to open that door no matter how scared I was.

On our way to registration, she asked me in a patient voice why it was I had disobeyed her. And when I looked up at her, I remember she looked back, and that once again we had come upon a silent agreement: I was not only strange, I was stupid.

It is one thing to enter a new school for the first time. It is another to come from an Eastern school and go to a Western one. Both are bad enough, especially when one has failed every subject including art. But it is even worse when one is not only frightened half to death by everything in life but quite aware of going slowly mad as well. A few days after registration, or perhaps it was weeks, I walked into my first class with my eyes closed. I remember well that uneasy moment when my history teacher, Miss Collingwood, a small and paper-thin woman who actually liked kids and whose every breath was filled with something to learn, introduced me to my new classmates, each and every one of whom smiled in welcome at the kid from Connecticut, population two and one-half million approximately, capitol Hartford, Nutmeg State, growers of tobacco and makers of guns and diggers of clams. And best of all I remember the election that was held on that first day to choose the class president for the rest of the year. Because I had come from so far away a place that they made guns there and grew tobacco and dug clams, and also because I looked so scared, I was instantly voted in on a landslide of upraised hands. I held that high office for three days. It was during the recess of the third day that I finally found the courage to go into the play-yard. All the girls were at one end playing tag. All the boys were at the other end choosing sides for baseball and arguing as to which team would get me. They would argue over me in future games too, but for the opposite reason. It was not so much, as they would soon learn, that I didn't know how to play baseball; they forgave me for that because of where I had come from, thinking that maybe that game wasn't played by the children of the East. And it was not the strange New England accent either, which they made fun of, but in a friendly way. It was me they didn't like, it was everything about me;

everything shook, my voice and my hands and my legs. I couldn't stop the shaking. I felt for sure that if I lost this one, I would never win another; and I lost beautifully. After a very short discussion, they put their ex-president in left field and every time a ball was hit my way, in that first game and in the few others, I would hear a loud groan from my team and a knowing cheer from the other long before I could even make myself move to run under the fast-descending balls I knew I would drop.

There were lots of other things about that school and school-year I didn't understand. One was the origin of the name of my new state that was pounded into all of us by that fifth grade teacher as if the state, like me, simply had to have something to hang onto, something concrete that wouldn't go away. The Kutenai, Nez Percé, Western Shoshone, Pend d 'Oreille, and Blackfoot Indians had long ago called their desert land Sun Coming over the Mountains, the sound of which was somehow twisted by the White Man into Idaho. We were made to memorize the names of every county from the Sawtooth Mountains to the Bitterroot and every historical twist and turn in the Lo Lo Trail that Lewis and Clark had traveled on. We were taught that fur trappers and trading-post builders and gold and silver seekers had perilously made their way down that same trail to bring to the Indians the gift of Civilization. We were taught the past histories of those Indian tribes, how they had lived and what they had made and who they had prayed to and how brave they had been, as if their history and their gods and their bravery were dead, as if hundreds of them didn't still live and pray in shacks made of boards and burlap and beer cans at the edge of town by the garbage dump in the desert. And sometimes, while trying to forget my problems, while trying to forget that father was now dying in a San Francisco Merchant Marine hospital that was found in a phonebook and that new mother and her old parents had finally persuaded him to die in, and that they had only taken me in because I was the son of a living father, I would go after the last school bell to the garbage dump in the desert and to the dirt roads around the shacks; and even though they hated me too because I was white and wearing clean clothes, I would pretend to be one of them, I would pretend to be an Indian in the Sun Coming over the Mountains.

I would walk on their roads when the sun was going down, slouched over and slow, my face burned into deep wrinkles by the sun and the wind, my mind wearing the buffalo skins that had been sewn with bone and gut when the hunting was good, my brave black eyes on the soft and quick brown hands of the daughter of the chief, hands that laugh golden in the sun and then jingle silver in the dark of my tent from the bracelets I'd given when the hunting was good; and with my face and mind and eyes, with every Indian inch of me shaking with long bright feathers, I would pretend not to see, or to show that I'd seen, the reality of the dirt and the hunger and the empty hours and the red glow in a dark doorway of an old man's pipe

shooting arrows of sparks into a black smoke of flies that circle his head and fall now and then as if shot to feed on the
belly of a child farther back in the darkness, so far back that
only her navel is seen, distended and swollen and red, glowing
like another pipe.

I think of that now, of my wishes and dreams that rode
horses, of the Indian shacks, of the new mother and town and
school, of the new everything in life that can be new, and of
a young boy some years later standing naked in the darkness of
his cell, others kneeling in front of him one by one, as if in
worship, taking turns like flies to feed on the only thing he
has left, distended and swollen and red, a meal that not even
screams would end had he the courage to scream; and the more
I think of him and of others like him and of all those years
that were different only because of the different people in them,
the more I realize that only our wishes and dreams were new
and that all else was a shared nightmare from which no one
ever awoke.

But I think too, and because I have to, that perhaps we all
had some chance that for some reason or other we never took,
some chance beyond dreams that we all could have taken to
make things better, to keep kids out of cells, to give Indians
something to do, to give father and new mother and me a big
lawn somewhere to be looked at from behind blue shutters.
Perhaps, had we been other people and living in some other
town, had it been a different year or had father not been sick,
had jobs and houses and friendship and other things been easier

to get, had there been no recent war needing merchant ships to help bring death to foreign ports and then passenger ships to bring visitors to see the death who would take some back home as souvenirs, had one or all of us in my family or in the families of others done something different in the right time or place, or had I not been me . . . . then perhaps many more of our wishes and dreams could have found blue shutters more easily, could have planted the gardens we wanted. But whatever that chance was, it was never taken; and nothing was right, not the people, not the time, not anything we did, not anything that was done to us. It had always been that way of course, but now I was ten, and old enough to see that others were suffering too, and old enough to know just how wrong everything was. The whole thing was wrong, the world, our lives, my Indians, and my father always sitting with a pale face in a dark chair by a silver bucket rung with spit.

The sun came, the sun went, father died, I inherited his watch and ring and foreign coin collection and then moved with new mother into a new apartment that was as far from her old parents' house and my father's memory as she could move us and across the street from a red brick library in a green park.

6

But before I go any further into that part of my life that I remember so well, my tenth year and our new apartment and the real beginning of the madness (and also the most horrible sentence I have ever heard in my life, when my fifth grade arithmetic teacher told our class that we would all stay pretty much the same mentally and emotionally throughout our lives as we were then), I first want to think of other childhood things. My memory is getting stronger now and I want to make use of it. There are many dark spaces still in my mind and I want them to go away. What was it that happened in my seventh year when my real mother came out of her bedroom after the moaning? And I remember my tenth year very well, though not how it ended, and some of the years that came after; but what was it that happened in the months and years I don't remember that was important enough for my mind to forget?

Memory . . . . the ability to think back on all those little deaths that one didn't die from . . . . without it we wouldn't be people, without it there wouldn't be any time, no yesterdays, todays, or tomorrows, no madness or sanity, no reasons for ever getting up in the mornings. Sometimes I stay in bed for as long as I can, at other times it is good to get up; some days I can easily think of something that happened five years ago, yet for my life I can't remember anything at all I did yesterday. But there is a reason for this; everything in life has a reason.

That something that happened five years ago has had a long time to come of age, it has been remembered over and over again, not the actual thing itself but the memories of it, the thousands of the forever-changing memories of it on top of a thousand more.

For instance . . . . one day, I think it was about five years ago, I met a girl on a New York street who I thought looked a little like my cousin Bobby in Connecticut, though I didn't tell her that, and after a short discussion about price we were on a bus and in my room. While she undressed, I remembered how we met, though that seems now to be a rather silly thing to be thinking about, and during at least some of the time we were in bed, I remembered the sights and the sounds of her undressing and most of what was said all the way down to her stockings which she insisted upon wearing. Then later, while she was struggling again with her tight-fitting work clothes and complaining about her station in life, I was able to remember almost everything that had taken place before . . . . how we had met, the pigeons in the park, the bus ride and the perfume and the people staring, her disappointment with my tiny room, the shock of the cold as all our clothes came off except for her stockings, the first touch and kiss and the softly violent sex with its coming and getting ready to go. An hour or so after she'd gone, I remembered it all again, the whole stupid thing from start to finish, though not so clearly, and probably jerked off. The next day, either while in my room or walking the streets, I thought of her again, not of her really but of the girl I had thought about while jerking off, and was sorry I hadn't been nicer to her. A month or so after that she came again into my mind and was even more changed, not like cousin Bobby at all, not like anybody I had ever met, clean black hair instead of smelly brown, and with a beautiful face. Years later it would not be her I would think about whenever the loneliness was a little too much, but any one of those thousands of lovely memories of her on top of a thousand more, each only a memory of the one that had come before. And now, a half a decade later, all about her is as confused as an old dream. Did this particular person really happen or did I just use the bits and pieces of other memories, or wishes, to make her up? Was it five years ago or only a few months? Was it a boy?

Memory is funny . . . . it's all there is, really . . . . and I try so hard not to let it lie to me . . . . I try so hard to replace vanity with truth and fear with reason . . . . and yet still, for all my searching, there are so many years I can't remember . . . . the end of my tenth year . . . . age eleven . . . . age twelve . . . . age thirteen . . . . all blank in my memory. But I do remember some things in each year. And I do remember that I finally ran away from somewhere . . . . but when, and where was it? And how did I ever get such courage? . . . I do remember the buses . . . . kept changing them every few towns so that nobody who was following me would find me. But as it turned out, nobody was . . . . Pocatello . . . . Des Moines . . . . Chicago . . . . I remember riding and riding

. . . . trying to get back to Connecticut . . . . a Negro lady on one bus singing and singing. And I remember walking for miles when my money gave out, sitting by the road for hours when my shoes gave out . . . . and sleeping for many warm nights on cold park benches . . . . and locked up somewhere for loitering . . . . my first jail . . . . my first fears as an adult . . . . no toilets in the cells, only buckets . . . . the smell of the shit of hundreds of prisoners . . . . my asthma coming back for the first time in years, as if to see if I was still there . . . . but powerful now, and lasting for years. And then somehow, after many months of fighting to breathe, I was put on a train that had toilets but no windows . . . . and I couldn't breathe at all. Nobody wanted me, and yet at the same time it seemed that everybody wanted me; why else would they bother to spend so much time in locking me up, taking me on trains, putting me in homes? . . . and they put me in my first children's home . . . . in Connecticut I think . . . . girls on the third floor . . . . boys on the second . . . . sex in the laundry room . . . . but there's a good clue to help my memory . . . . sex . . . . everybody remembers where they were and how old they were on their first sex day . . . . what happened that first time? . . . who helped to make it happen? . . . was it anything to write home about?

Sex . . . . but for really, really the first time. I am either eight or nine or ten. My next-door neighbor is either eight or nine or ten. I have been trying to play with him for weeks, with his dog, with his erector set, with his BB gun, with anything at all of his just so I can stop being, even if only for a day or two, the only kid in town with never ever anything to do.

The sun is walking through leaves. I am standing on the sidewalk in front of his house, pretending to be watching a tree but watching instead out of one eye's corner his house, his blue bike leaning against the steps, and his small dog with its white tail always in the air.

The front door opens. The wind blows warm on my face. Without even glancing at the door I stare as hard as I can at the tree, hoping beyond all other things that the next time I look it will be the boy. The leaves of the tree are many. Curious how they touch each other and flap away and close and open the sun. Thousands of them, and of all colors of yellow and green.

The boy's mother goes to the large silver can a few feet away and dumps in the bag of garbage. I glance at her and smile so she won't think I'm crazy. She glances back while closing the noisy lid, then walks back to the house.

I shift my weight to the other eye and the other foot, tired of watching leaves, and I watch the house while listening to the dog as it trots over and sniffs at the newly fed can, then looks up at me and growls softly with its throat. Now I watch the dog, pretending that everything dogs do is of great importance to me. I become an expert on the habits of dogs. It goes to a bush, lifts its leg while looking at me, and pees in a straight yellow line. It goes over to something in the grass and eats it, licks its smiling lips and goes up to the steps to sit, comes back down the steps after a long sit and digs a hole in some flowers, goes back to the wet bush and sniffs, smiles up at me again as if what it was smelling was something I did, and maybe it was, laughs a little to itself and sits and scratches.

Another warm wind on my face and the front door opens again. I shift my weight again, my eyes float all over the place, looking at the dog, at the tree, at the cars falling down the street, at everything, at nothing. The boy walks down the steps; I can hear his small shoes on the wood, on the grass, on the light in the tree. The dog goes crazy. I've never heard or seen a dog go so crazy before. The boy sits with a thumping plop in the grass and that dog jumps all over him, laughing and telling him about how I peed on their bush. I pretend with all of my mind and body that I'm not looking or listening. I feel the blood pounding in my face. My arms lock to my wooden sides. The sidewalk beneath me melts and my feet sink in and the cement around them hardens and my eyes that are filled with the sun in the leaves start to bulge with pain. Then, either on that day or on some one of the dozens before it or after, the boy comes all the way over to me; I can hear his shoes and his dog walking on the grass, a distance of miles. He thinks it funny that I am always standing outside his house, he laughs when I tell him I like his tree and that I've been watching his dog all this time because I've been thinking about buying the same breed. He thinks everything about me is funny, and maybe he's right. He thinks there might be something wrong with me, and maybe there is. I agree with everything he says. We go into his garage to play doctor. The feeling of happiness is so strange. I smell gasoline and oil. I see barrels and boxes of rags and stacks of firewood. We undress. My large eyes watch his hands as they find nothing wrong with me at all. Then suddenly the doors to our garage slam open and the fire goes out. His father has the widest mouth I have ever seen. The dog runs out. Time stops. No sound. Only the wind in a tree. I never did get to play with his BB gun.

Sex . . . . first kiss . . . . I don't remember the age . . . . with a girl from my class and down the block . . . . a tomboy called Billie or something, and in Connecticut I think, maybe somewhere else. There's a tent in my backyard . . . . I don't remember where I got that tent, probably stole it, a pup tent, the small and low kind the Boy Scouts use to get close in while discussing merit badges on cool evenings . . . . I smell canvas, grass, dirt, wood poles, newly smeared lipstick . . . . we kiss for an hour or more, making loud smacking sounds. I try my best to do it like they do it in the movies. But there isn't any music. Nothing is real. She tastes like bubble gum. Our kisses get louder and louder. We don't care who hears them. We want the entire world to know she's not the tomboy everybody thinks, and that I'm not what they think either. We lie side by side on the cold ground, the closed mouth in my excited head rising in the air again and again to come down on hers for smack after smack. Our arms are spread in a cross, not moving, nailed arm on arm like wood to wood. Our bodies are the same, but not touching, we've not learned that yet, rigid and as tight to the ground as the tent pegs. Then suddenly, both in the same smacking moment, we realize that everything is all wrong, that we're doing nothing right, and we stop, our mouths too sore to continue anyway. Without a word she leaves my tent to climb a tree. I stay for a while and try to remember what it was in all those movies that should have come next. I listen to the heavy breathing I'd forgotten to use and to the soft sneakers scraping on branches, and then I wipe my mouth, get up, and go home.

Sex . . . . the music begins now . . . . the calmness that for a long time I would think only I had discovered . . . . the silent sanity that began at pretty much the same time as the madness . . . . so loud and beautiful sometimes that I could not and cannot think or breathe. I discovered my body long before anyone else had a chance to, spoke to it for hours with my hands . . . . at age ten I think . . . . yes, my room is very nice in my memory, and the curtains have been pulled as dark as sleep because I have the measles . . . . lovely disease . . . . an orchestra has played it on my body . . . . no fifth grade for two whole weeks. Scab after bloody brown scab grows beneath my fingernails when I pick . . . . the quiet listening to the body as the nails scrape and dig . . . . the salty taste of the body as the nails are cleaned with sharp teeth . . . . the pleasure of the feeling from fingers to skin to eyes, mouth, and mind . . . . the feeling that finally the body has joined the mind in a sickness that will not be easy to cure. I am spotted like a leopard and I growl softly while thinking of many things . . . . a kangaroo splashing through mud, a snake I once saw crawling over pebbles by the Snake River, footprints I had made in the sand, sunlight spotting the water, ants melted to the hot sand like red sugar, a splatter-painting I once made using brown water colors and a green toothbrush . . . . that snake was green and I had smashed it with a rock . . . . sometimes I kill things. Sometimes I leave my warm bed and walk barefoot through the measle-darkness of my cold floor and go up to the dark curtains to open up the rest of the world and say—c'mon in, I've something to show you. And then I show that something to the sun, while examining closely the many tiny wonders I dig from my body . . . . and then I stare with all of the eyes of my mind and body deep into the light of the sun for long blinding seconds.

Sex . . . . I am about eleven in my memory now . . . . and we must be outside because the cold is much different . . . . yes, and it must be night, for it is very hard to see . . . . especially without all the white lights of the green dayroom ceiling of my first insane asylum . . . . my eyes are taking their time in getting used to the darkness. The first thing I see is the bright yellow flame being poured from the red can of gasoline . . . . then the social worker steps back, her eyes and teeth smiling in the light of the fire . . . . and now we all move forward in a tight group like little frightened soldiers uniformed neatly in Civil War gray, our hands holding franks

and sticks and marshmallows . . . . and we roast and eat and
stand around quietly, staring at the warm and pretty fire . . . .
no sound, except for the nice crackling and popping of the
logs, leaves, and sticks . . . . no movement, except for the
flames and smoke, and the few brave ones of us who dare to go
back to the wall to get more food from the baskets. We eat our
burned franks and lick away the sweet stickiness of the melted
sugar, and we wait where we stand, most of us, for the brave
ones to come back with more food for us to burn and eat. I
look around, my eyes seeing better now, courageous in the dark
where no one can see my shaking. The shadows dance on the
red brick walls, and on the sharp wires on top of the tall silver
fence that surrounds our play-yard, and on the faces of the kids
. . . . faces ugly enough even in daylight, but old and horrible
now like those of monsters . . . . and their shadows too, moving from side to side on the cold ground and bending up on
the brick in back of us all the way to the third floor, are different and larger and not shadows of kids. The thought that I
must look the same to them, and that they can see the monsters
in me, frightens me and my hands begin to shake so hard that
I drop my roasting stick . . . . but I think and I think, and
remember good things, and the shaking stops . . . . I look
back to the brick, my eyes climbing over the shadows from
floor to floor . . . . from the dark windows of the nursery,
kitchen, and storeroom to the white and empty windows of
our floor to the burning glass of the third floor where the
faces of the adults, too old to join the party, are staring down
at us . . . . then my eyes get tired and fall back to the fire

. . . . and now, one of our social workers, uneasy at the silence of children who aren't having as good a time as she thinks they should, claps her hands to get our attention. —Let's all sing, she says. And now finally there is a little life to our party, some laughter, a few voices and giggles, the sound of the feet of the braver ones kicking at embers . . . . but all these sounds are broken at the ends, muffled by the strangeness of actually being out in the play-yard for the first time ever at night. And I know, as most of the others know, that it would be the easiest thing in the world in this blackness to slip away unseen and go over to the fence and climb with the fingers of hands and the toes of shoes in silver holes, inches and inches up and then over, to land quietly in the weeds on the other side. I of course don't have the kind of courage it takes to jump the fence, but there are those of us who do, those I've heard talk about it in whispers at night . . . . I study those faces now, while humming a song about a rabbit that some social worker has insisted we sing even though none of us know the words . . . . I hum and stare hard at the bright shadows, hoping and praying that maybe the darkness and the fire might give at least one or two of them the final courage to go home. I see one look around and then another, their faces lit by more than fire. I watch their shoes, knowing that at any minute those will be the first to move . . . . and now some social worker is telling us the song has ended . . . . our voices shut, the humming and the mumbling stops, we listen to the fire. —Let's all dance, a social workers tells us in a voice that seems pleased by the success of the last game. We form a large circle around the fire, our hands holding the other hands on each side of us, and we dance . . . . our circle moving first one way and then the other. I turn my head to look back to the third-floor windows . . . . the adults, one alone at each bright window, and just over the bouncing shadows of our own heads, are moving with us, swaying from side to side. I face the fire again, pulled and pushed by all the hands, and as I dance I look from foot to dancing foot, and to each of the hand-held hands that I can see . . . . and I wait for the touch that will somewhere be broken . . . . I know it will . . . . I just know it . . . . and then, and just as suddenly as it all started, nothing happens . . . . the feet stay where they have stopped, the dance has ended, the fire is going out, the play-yard time is over, our fingers are untangling, and we are all lining up in double file to march back to our ward. I look to my partner, one of my heroes, one of the older boys I had expected so much of. His face is covered with excuses, but also with anger. He looks up at the brick in front of us and then bends down to pick up a rock . . . . I look up . . . . way above the top of our doorway, and behind one of the windows of the third floor, there is one last face staring down, the body beneath it crouched naked and hairy on a table and close to the glass. —Go ahead, I whisper to the boy. Our line begins to move toward the light of the open door. —One, two, three, four, the social workers are counting . . . . the face of the boy seems uglier in the door light than it was in the fire. —Go ahead, throw it, I whisper. —Five, six, seven, eight, nine, ten, the social workers are counting . . . . then the rock falls, silent and harmless in the dirt, and we are all through the door, our footsteps marching up the steel stairs. Behind us the play-yard door slams on its heavy lock . . . . the night is shattered.

Sex . . . . many months later . . . . age twelve I think . . . . or may be much older . . . . my memory has fallen apart almost as badly as my shoes . . . . my mind is as empty as my pockets. The roar of the buses is still in my ears . . . . I've jumped the fence and taken many buses and walked and walked for miles. There was a man at a hot dog stand some miles back . . . . he was so lonely that when he started to talk to me he couldn't stop . . . . he talked and talked and all I did was listen. Sometimes I would nod or say yes or no, but he didn't seem to know or care that I hadn't understood a word he had said . . . . later, after a quick taxi ride, and in his small room that had a tree growing in the window, he undressed me and spoke to me again with his mouth and with his hands . . . . it was then that I began to hear him.

Sex . . . . a different kind of freedom . . . . three or four years later I think . . . . a basement room in a roominghouse in any one of a dozen or more towns and cities in any one of many states. A wobbly table, a lightbulb in a ceiling sick with age and decay, an angry closet with banging hangers, a hot and rain-fed air that can't be sucked, madness and a bed . . . . on the bed there is me, naked as a birthday and ten times as hungry, listening to the sounds of the rain and the horrible wheezing. Asthma has crippled me from going to work, or from looking for work to go to, as a movie usher, truck loader, dish washer, or factory sweeper. Either that or laziness . . . . the sound of the sucking at the air is like kisses . . . . I haven't worked, washed, changed clothes, gone to church, or eaten for many days . . . . the room smells, the bed smells, I smell . . . . I get the feeling, while lying here with my body sweating dirt and with my lungs lying dead within me like two broken balloons, that something is very wrong with my life, and that everything about me is dead. But no, not everything; there is still one thing that is quite alive . . . . beside me on the wet sheets there are two piles of ripped-out pictures, one from *Playboy* and the other from *Good House-keeping* . . . . and as I've done several times before on this day, and on many of the days before it, and as I will do several times more on this day and for many days after, I stare for long hours at picture after picture of naked girls and plates of food . . . . and with all the power of my eyes, hands, mind, and body I enter the pictures, become a living part of what I want and need the most . . . . I touch and grab at the flesh of the beautiful girls, eat the sandwiches and puddings and the little blue cakes with their red and white icings . . . . and I begin to enjoy the pain, and the torture becomes as much a part of me as does my wanting for it to end. And even though I can't breathe, with the air all around me hot with rain falling on green leaves, I almost succeed in doing it; I come very close to winning the battle I had begun at the age of ten, that of pretending I can get what I want by just wishing . . . . and I cover the pictures again and

again with myself . . . . jerking and pulling at my mind and
body . . . . begging out all of the strength of my insides . . . .
freeing the madness . . . . erupting and hurting into the hot
wet air white and thick like icing.

Sex . . . . years later . . . . I am twenty-three . . . .
everything's the same. I'm in a different room, in a different
city, in a different state, and my asthma has taken a vacation
and won't be back until spring. But except for these things,
everything's the same . . . . the same kind of room and bed,
the same madness, magazines, dirt, and hunger . . . . and in-
between my many moments of making love to myself I sleep
for as many hours as I can . . . . then wake and love and sleep
again. Then suddenly, one cold afternoon, I hear shouting from
my window and dress and go outside . . . . and in either a
wastebasket or a gutter, I forget which, I find a newspaper that
says a president has just been shot and killed . . . . I read for
a while as I walk down the street, then throw the paper away,
thinking only about getting something to eat for the first time
in days, and not caring how I get it. Years later, in other rooms
in other cities, I would read about others getting shot, and I
would compare my life to those of the assassins, and sometimes
I would find a remarkable similarity . . . . and I would think
about that.

Sex . . . . the music grows louder. It thunders in my head
sometimes with small memories that didn't matter at the time;

at other times the music is soft and nice to listen to even though when it was first played, it was deadly . . . . I am somewhere in my early teens now . . . . and living in one of my several children's homes that came somewhere in-between my first two insane asylums . . . . I am beginning to remember things now . . . . the mind is the safest place to keep anything . . . . and I have kept everything, my whole life, if only I can find the important things. I remember many dark doorways where children stared in pajamas . . . . room after room of white silent eyes . . . . thick doors with round wooden peep holes where the hungry hands at the ends of dirty pajamas grabbed each morning at the bread and butter of breakfast . . . . cold empty bathrooms with warm dripping radiators and yellow urinals of burning water . . . . the Juvenile Courtrooms downstairs where the wrinkled judges sat in big black chairs, fat and safe in the protective purity of their long black robes, giving freely of their time . . . . and social workers in these places too, young and pretty, giving kind words and comic books . . . . and the guards upstairs wearing smiles and black leather belts with painful buckles and silver keys . . . . and the tiny kitchen of my floor where the butter is spread thickly on the newly baked bread and placed neatly on the carefully scrubbed and gleaming trays . . . . and the dumbwaiter, clanking and crawling up to our kitchen from the big kitchen that is steaming away somewhere in the basement . . . . up it comes to the first floor of the toys, paper dolls, and painted horses of the twelves and under . . . . up and up it comes as I listen to the music. It passes my kitchen to visit the third floor where the girls of all ages live and sew and cry . . . . now I hear the metal doors being opened and crashed closed again. I stand at the metal sink, washing the metal trays, pouring hot water, scrubbing with steel, drying and stacking . . . . I pull the plug and the water whirls toward the drain and I dry my hands, listening for the clank and crawl of the dumbwaiter. It jumps to a stop at my floor and I use both hands to pry open the silver doors and reach in to pick from the grease the letters of love that I know were written by any one of the girls upstairs to any one of us boys downstairs who might happen to be washing dishes at the time. The doors crash closed under the weight of no hands to hold them . . . . I unfold the letters and read the scribbled words slowly, always knowing when I do that all of my life has been worth it. I write my own on napkins, the white ones of my floor rather than the pink ones of upstairs, and I never sign them . . . . then I open the doors and throw them in and push the red button and listen to the clank and the crawl of my letters going up and up, almost so far up that God might read them. Then, while listening to the faint sounds falling down the metal shaft, I do with their letters what I know the faceless ones above me are doing with mine . . . . and later I send their wet ones back . . . . and they send back mine.

I'm in my bed trying to sleep. It is always difficult to sleep in the dormitory . . . . small shadows touch on barefoot tile

. . . . children pray and play on knees and feet and between warm covers . . . . the patter of little feet . . . . the chatter of big mouths if I should ever be caught doing the same thing. The aisles are quickly crossed . . . . the sounds are small and muffled . . . . the night guard, a stupid and sleepy man named Mr. Portamonte, is snoring from his office many dark beds and corners away. I listen . . . . my ears are alive . . . . and so are my hands. All of us are issued brown blankets from the same closet each night, but no one ever gets the same one twice. I know this because I don't care much for any of the boys down here and can't get at any of all those girls above, so I have to jerk off alone in my dirty brown blanket of that night, and I always remember just which part of each night's blanket was the lucky part and never once have I ever gotten any of them back . . . . mostly I think of the girls, of their faces and bodies I have never seen, and of our wet letters of love that we lick . . . . but sometimes, while feeling with my fingers my body and blanket, and while listening to all the lonely little sounds of my dormitory, I pull at myself and try to imagine just who is doing what to whom in the darkness . . . . and I try to think of who it might be tonight who is being blessed at this moment by my dirty blanket of last night, or warmed by all those other blankets I've come in.

My dormitory has been filled with new arrivals, car stealers, rock throwers, candy bar takers, school truants and runaways, mostly black kids, a few Puerto Ricans, two whites, and one six-foot-tall kid of unknown race who wears a dress. To make room for all these law-breakers, I have been moved to a private room. It is night now . . . . blackness is between the bars of my window. I've already checked my brown blanket of tonight . . . . found nothing. I listen now . . . . the girls above me and my fellow roomers are pressing their faces into the bars of their windows, whispering in careful voices to the rooms below. Some of us are whispering back, others are quiet, like me, waiting for the little kids in the cells below us to get up the courage to leave their small beds and join into the conversations being whispered and giggled into the night. I grasp the bars of my window and wait. And now, one by one, mostly boys, and among the hard sounds of us male and female convicts, the tiny voices of children are heard . . . . then it happens . . . . the main event of the late evening . . . . the moment that most of us have been waiting for. There are no commands . . . . there is no one single person who all of a sudden shouts—hey, let's all pee on the little kids . . . . it just happens. Suddenly there it is, twenty or so warm bodies pressed to the cold bars, a torrent of golden rain flowing down the bricks, down to the laughter of the little fingers of the first floor.

I remember now . . . . I was working in the laundry in the basement, separating all the dirty clothes into small neat piles that were labeled by a metal marker nailed to the brick with the words, girls, boys, children . . . . the laundry lady, a big black hunk of the outside life, had her big black head safely tucked through the door of one of the white machines. A girl about my age walked in from the kitchen next door. She wore a blue uniform, her black hair shone in the light of the ceiling bulbs, her hands were red from peeling beets or something, her eyes were as brown as earth and wet from looking at onions. . . . Yes, that's it . . . . I remember it now. It was in that laundry room that I did it first . . . . she smiled and I smiled and the white walls with all those white rumbling machines moved close and suddenly we were stuck in a corner, wrestling on top of a pile of dirty underwear. We kissed without smacking, our arms and legs went crazy, neither of us had seen a young sex of the opposite for months . . . . I somehow got my pants down . . . . we both tore hers off . . . . I almost had it in when the black laundry lady looked up and the ceiling came down . . . . her screams entered into the poundings and the crashings of the machines, and I almost had it in when my new friend kneed me hard in the balls, pulled up her pants, and went calmly back to her onions.

I can remember now what happened when my real mother came out . . . . she opened the bedroom door and I ran toward that door faster than I've ever run before or since . . . . and I remember that the smell from the shit on the back of her dress didn't really matter . . . . and we stood there for a while just looking, with silly grins on our faces, and then she said—c'mon, let's fuck . . . . and that's what we did.

Sex . . . . New York or Boston or Atlanta or Baltimore or Tampa or Miami . . . . I am anywhere from fourteen to eight-een or so . . . . and standing in front of a bookstore, always a bookstore, on Broadway or Collins Avenue or Peach Street or Main Street . . . . he smiles . . . . I smile . . . . a match is lit . . . . I am very hungry and we agree on price and go up to my room . . . . or to his room . . . . or we don't agree on price but go anyway . . . . both of us in bed . . . . a person can get used to almost anything . . . . he tries and tries with his mouth, his Star of David dangling between my legs . . . . the disgust may be gone but I'm too tired . . . . finally he gives up on me and decides to do it to himself . . . . I relax now . . . . my eyes play with the ceiling . . . . the pain is gone now . . . . soft music . . . . lights low . . . . very romantic . . . . he pulls and pulls at his fat ugly body . . . . the veins pop out on his old head beneath white hair . . . . I stare at an empty bottle, at the black telephone, at the heavy lamp . . . . I almost get up the courage to pick up one or all of those things and pound and smash them into that horrible head . . . . then finally he succeeds . . . . but he comes blood . . . . my God, he comes blood.

Sex . . . . on another street . . . . or in any one of my dozens of furnished rooms. But are all these things important enough for me to think about? Am I just wasting my time? . . . yes they are and no I'm not . . . . because I must remember what happened to the ten-year-old, and because even when I was alone, I was never really alone . . . . there were hundreds all around me all the time whose childhoods fixed the rest of their lives . . . . perhaps thousands . . . . seldom speaking to each other, constantly trying to forget or to remember either our

tenth year on earth or some other year, wandering from town
to town and street to street and children's home to furnished
room to jail to asylum . . . . millions maybe . . . . fighting,
drinking, trying to figure things out . . . . the hunger was fantastic . . . . day after violent day with nothing to eat . . . .
police everywhere . . . . how many does it take to guard one
doughnut, a tunafish sandwich, a can of warm beer? . . . stole
a quart bottle of prune juice once after days of not eating . . . .
drank the whole thing . . . . never do that again . . . . got
into a fight once in a bar in Boston . . . . one of dozens in one
of hundreds . . . . Playland was the name of it I think . . . .
me and another guy . . . . we fought with fists and then with
chairs and bottles . . . . his friends joined in and then the people who knew me . . . . we wrecked the place and each other
. . . . blood everywhere . . . . on my head, on his face, on our
clothes . . . . then when the cops came we said what the hell
and made friends and went up to my room . . . . or to his
room . . . . we slept together that night in a bed of blood . . . .
what the hell . . . . then in the morning we awoke to find ourselves still alive, still hungry . . . . and the music continued
. . . . almost enough beer and cheap booze to drown in . . . .
but never quite enough . . . . beer, booze, benzedrine, dexe-
drine, seconals, tuinals, amyl nitrate, phenobarbital, sodium
pentothal, methadrine, cocaine, yellow jackets, black beauties,
ethyl, snappers, codeine, millions of bad movies . . . . and an
occasional bright liquid poppy flower dreaming in a glass tube.
—Keep a stiff upper lip, someone once told me. But how is that
possible when the one under it is forever trembling? . . . I re-

member once entering a small grocery store with my two best and only friends I had met that morning at a Salvation Army breakfast . . . . juice, coffee, and toast doesn't stay with one for very long, and our stomachs are growling at the world . . . . we are ready to kill. We stand around for a while looking at all the shelves of unreachable food . . . . comparing the prices of tunafish. When the store is empty of customers we go up to the man and his iron cash register . . . . he already seems to sense that something is wrong . . . . something is. His store is open, his mouth is open, his cash register is slammed closed. I feel the bulge of the Belgian automatic in my coat . . . . I see my two friends staring at me, waiting for me to be served first . . . . I hear the man asking—yes, yes, yes? . . . over and over he asks—yes, yes, yes? . . . but my hands and feet get scared and I can't do it . . . . why does it always have to be me who carries the gun? . . . I walk out without looking back. Later I put a five-cent stamp on the gun and drop it into an empty mailbox where it bangs on the bottom and I go up to my room and undress and then feel all the pressure of the day's hunger build and flood in my excited fingers . . . . still later, and in one of a city of bars, I hear that my two friends robbed the man anyway, peeing on his floor and stealing several cans of tunafish.

Sex . . . . I am anywhere from fifteen to twenty-five and in any one of a number of barred places . . . . I can't remember how many, or how many times in each . . . . Tampa City Jail,

Baltimore City Prison, Hackensack City Jail, Rikers Island, Harts Island, Annendale, Jamesburg, Manhattan House of Detention for Men . . . . in any one of many tombs . . . . the enormous years . . . . childhood without end . . . . the confusion when sanity and insanity get together and become one . . . . under lock and key for things I both did and didn't do . . . . tiers of cells with the tears of men that reach up to the high yellow ceiling . . . . catwalks and long winding stairs . . . . the constant flushing of toilets so powerful they've been known to swallow men . . . . iron locks that tickle, clang, and slam . . . . power-mad guards prowling like cats on loud pig feet, jangling their thick silver rings of keys . . . . golden gongs playing with our minds when all the bells ring . . . . hidden radios blaring from the Outside with rock and roll and war news . . . . our side is winning . . . . nights with wide eyes and days with nothing to see . . . . the wings of gray pigeons flapping at the barred windows and at the flaw in my character . . . . our side is winning . . . . the stink of the buckets and the yellow soap, the stink of the black and white and yellow jailbirds, the gray mops and buckets and white toilets, and the overflowing of everything, and the stink of men in cages with blocks of thick wood in their open and bloody mouths that are tightly screwed to the backs of their shaved heads by tiny stainless steel plates all exactly three-quarters of an inch thin . . . . or was it all just a dream? . . .

I am in my cell, which is numbered 9UB6 on the pink card I must always carry, and on my bunk, the paper-thin mattress of which is fattened by many months of *Christian Science Monitors*, trying to sleep, trying not to listen to the early night noise of hundreds of men who are in their cells not trying to sleep . . . . the name of my cellmate is King Leong . . . . he once showed me his pink card . . . . he is a Chinaman and very old and can't walk very well. He is locked up for doing something with opium but since he has never taken the trouble to learn English, neither I nor the ones who locked him up can find out just exactly what it was. He is now sitting on the bunk above me with his legs dangling down, the yellow feet of which are only a few inches from my pillow. All his years of opium have gone to those legs and they are as yellow as father's spit had been when I was ten and fat with pus and falling apart, but I don't say anything because he keeps me supplied with cigarettes. It is almost time for lights-out and radio-off now, and almost all the men in our section are making up for all the noise they didn't or couldn't make during the day . . . . bars are being pounded with stolen cups . . . . shouts and screams are echoed back and forth between the metal walls . . . . the toilets are going crazy . . . . a boy named Barry, who was once my cell-mate, is crying softly two tiers down behind the padded bars of the Punishment Cell . . . . another boy, in the cell next to mine, is whimpering under the nightly rape of a mighty Negro named Spud . . . . the main gate down the hall on the first tier, two Punishment Cells away from Barry, is slammed closed. This slamming is the signal the guards use each night at this time to warn us that all our uncivilized noise must come to a final stop in exactly ten minutes. The men hear it and know that the lights and radio will soon join them in death, and to prove that they are still alive their shouting and pounding and flushing grows into a fever . . . . from the top to the bottom our entire jail of animals seem to shake with a sickness . . . . then something very strange happens . . . . it will last for hours and ends it . . . . in the bunk above me my Chinaman is singing . . . . in a sing-song hypnotic chant, low and strange like soft leaves brushing against tiny bells, King Leong's breath leaves our cell and travels to a hundred others . . . . the men are beginning to listen . . . . the final toilet of the night is flushed . . . . the last cup drops . . . . Barry has stopped crying . . . . even the rape has ended . . . . cell by cell and then section by section, all the men are quiet . . . . even the guards are listening.

My memory is now beginning to roar at me like a river . . . . but surely I am past drowning after all this time . . . . and surely there is no need to clutch at straws anymore . . . . I am getting to the truth . . . . I am not so afraid anymore . . . . I am winning . . . . there were two insane asylums . . . . in my childhood, anyway . . . . lots later on, but only two then . . . . I remember that now for a fact . . . . the first swallowed me in the cold December of my tenth year . . . . the second in the summer of my fifteenth . . . . I keep thinking there were six or seven . . . . but there were only two . . . . and only one trip to each . . . . even though it sometimes seems that's all I did in my childhood . . . . travel quiet in fast black cars to and from stone places, sit quiet on cold car seats while watching through thick windows as the different people waved good-bye, sit quiet on wooden chairs or green metal benches while eating cold food, lie quiet on strange beds while watching the walls sweat and the bugs coming out to drink and the mice coming out to eat the bugs, sit or lie quiet on tile or concrete floors in gray stone or green metal dayrooms while only my eyes moved and only my fingers spoke . . . . sit quiet with all my thoughts . . . . so many that not even God could count them . . . . sit quiet in the childhood of my life . . . . while waiting to grow up . . . . while seeing and listening and learning with the eyes, ears, and mind of an animal growing stronger . . . . sit quiet . . . . do lots of other things, but above all don't cause trouble . . . . sit quiet.

But when will there be an end to this? . . . to all this searching? . . . how can I find the answers when I'm not even sure of the questions? . . . I feel like a spelunker without a light . . . . how much deeper must I go? . . . one hundred and twenty miles . . . . age ten . . . . my first trip . . . . clear, clean windows with miles of shining desert in them . . . . not many towns . . . . a black station wagon going ninety miles an hour in the wet white snow for one hundred and twenty miles . . . . I watched the speedometer most of the time . . . . fell asleep during the last half of the trip . . . . but I'll think about that first place later . . . . what does it matter which one I think of first anyway, all cages are the same . . . . all mental hospitals are the same. I am at some frightened age going to an insane asylum somewhere in some state and for some reason . . . . everything in life has a reason . . . . a purpose to everything under Heaven . . . . cloudy memories with skies crying on that first trip . . . . wet windows . . . . new mother or new somebody else waving good-bye . . . . I did not wave back . . . . got to give myself credit for that . . . . a black station wagon both times, I think . . . . the same kind of car and the same pretending and wishing that the ten-year-old shared with the fifteen-year-old . . . . the same two men saying—get in quick, we have to lock the doors, we have to put the children away . . . . they didn't really say that of course . . . . I don't think they ever said anything at all . . . . it's all the same really . . . . two Charons in white, driving me fast across the Snake or the Hackensack or the Styx . . . . crossing the Rivers of Forgetfulness . . . . it's all the same . . . . at age ten or at age fifteen the same fear is there . . . . the same iron bars separating the front seat from the back, the sane from the crazy . . . . on the first trip we made a stop in Boise to pick up a woman in a black dress . . . . on the second trip there were no stops . . . . I pretended for a long time on that first trip that the woman in the black dress was not sitting beside me, and that we had not stopped on a dark Boise sidestreet filled with snow, and that we had not gone into the dark hallway of a house, and that we had not dragged out a screaming woman as all the people watched frowning from all the windows . . . . and then later I pretended that she was my friend . . . . on the second trip there were no stops for women in black dresses . . . . we went fast through the streets of Hackensack, Passaic, Newark, Elizabeth . . . . and then southward on highways and in the mud of country roads . . . . and I saw lots of people, normal people, walking around quiet . . . . and I pretended lots of things with some of the pretty girls I saw . . . . some normal and some not so normal . . . . things that I would probably be locked up for if anyone ever found out about them . . . . and I pretended hard on the first trip, before I fell asleep, that my friend in the black dress was not spitting white drops on our floor, was not banging her head softly against our window, was not so totally different from me . . . . and I pretended on both trips that nothing had changed, that the world was all right, that there was no past, that the future would always be the same . . . . and in some ways I was right.

Age fifteen and also sixteen in New Jersey . . . . the music of insanity has drums and horns and six levels . . . . I've hit upon almost every single level like a ball bouncing up stairs. Level One is on the first floor, with its reception desk and its pretty nurses who never leave it once they've taken away your watch and ring and belt and your lucky stone with the funny white stripes . . . . and also its row of black telephones that speak only when spoken to, its glass gift counter with the little cloth toys and the tin-plate souvenirs hand-stamped and painted blue and silver, or gold if you like, by the inmates on the lower floors, its coffee shop where you can be served cake by the cream of the inmates, its air-conditioned visiting area with black tables and soft chairs and the occasional visitors for the extremely sane or lucky sometimes on Sundays, its public bathrooms kept shiny and clean, quite unlike the more private ones deeper in the building, its doctors' offices marked *Private* in black letters that were painted by the same inmates who make the souvenirs, and its heavy wood doors near the reception desk that have no marks, not even from fingernails, and that open sometimes to the Outside where the green lawn is and the sprinkler system that feeds it and the parking lot that feeds our building and also the small stream that I remember with all those white ducks . . . .

Level Two is on the second floor, with its babies in pink and blue cribs on Ward A; when they get a little older, they don't even have to leave the building, they can pick up their toys and cross the hall with its pictures of elephants and kangaroos and move right into Ward B, which is for all ages below twelve, and whenever they get tired enough of that ward and old and sane enough to go Outside and then don't quite make it, there is always Ward C on the same floor, where they can visit for a while with the men and women alcoholics and others and walk and crawl with them for hours and days and months around the tv's and the card games and the ping pong tables.

Level Three is on the third floor, with its kids over twelve and up to sixteen, its men at another end, and its women at a third, all of them living and dying for months and sometimes years in a triangle that is only slightly mad.

Level Four is on the fourth floor and is reserved for those adults who are not quite mad enough for Levels Five or Six, yet at the same time, not quite sane enough to go fooling around downstairs among a population where even one real nut could ruin their whole outlook on life.

Level Five is the quietest floor and also the smelliest, only the very peaceful are allowed in, the wetters, the moaners, the shit-eaters, the thumb-suckers, the vegetables with rotting skin, the Christs, and all the other do-nothings-ever of society. Except for Level Six, it is the maddest floor and the one that is the most difficult to leave. . . .

I live on Level Six.

There is a dayroom here as on the other floors, but ours is never used. When we aren't sleeping in our rooms under our blankets of many colors, we can usually be found either walking the hall or sitting in it on green metal benches. Sometimes, whenever the thought moves us, we use our fingernails to scratch things in the green paint . . . . lines, circles, crosses, naked bodies nailed to crosses, cocks and cunts smashed on crosses, our names, our numbers, our lives. And when we're not walking, or sitting and scratching, or mashing with our fingers or slippers the cockroaches or the occasional little black beetles into whatever or whoever is closest so as to listen for the cries, we are eating, sleeping, doing the various crazy things that sent us here, washing the floors or mopping the walls free of the shit and piss and food and mashed bugs, or painting over and over the many years of the scratches on our benches. I am the only one who has gone through all the layers of paint with my nails. No one else seems to care. I can go all the way down to the metal, through the soft stuff to the hard to the very hard to the first pictures and writings of years ago. These scratchings are the most interesting of all and the most difficult to clean, but nobody ever believes me anymore when I tell of what I find. And nobody ever seems to care. . . .

On one of the walls of the shock room there is a crack from the ceiling to the floor. Most of it flows downward like a river, wide in the valleys of dust and thin and narrow over the heat-bubble bumps of mountains, straight and deep and clean, as if cut by a razor. Other parts of this crack, with tiny islands of green paint breaking away, are jagged and dirty, as if the razor slipped. Many thin streams run from each island, so many that the counting of them is never the same, so many that all numbers, fingers, wires, thoughts, and strands of brown hair fuse together whenever the barred window turns to the sun, making the mountains and the streams and the valleys into a shadow of death. . . .

There's not much to do here. When the food cart comes slamming through the main doors, I am always the first to get into line. If I didn't, then nobody else would either. Everybody always watches me to see if I'm going to get up. Perhaps some-day I won't, and then nobody else will either and we'll all just sit on our benches and starve. . . .

They never tell you when they're coming, when it's your turn; I guess that's part of the shock. You can be walking around or scratching on the benches or whispering to some-body, and then all of a sudden it just happens and you wish to God it could be somebody else. As in everything else in life, there are certain stages through which you must first be pushed. The first stage is when the main doors open and it isn't even lunchtime. You hide a little behind your clothes and your hands and you think to yourself that maybe it's some kind of a pack-age coming through that some parent or uncle of an inmate sent but was too heavy to be carried by the usual Wednesday mail, a cake perhaps, or cookies, or comic books . . . . then you remember how seldom this happens. You think that perhaps it's a change of shift, some attendant got sick, something differ-ent in the dull routine of the day . . . . but no, that's not it. Maybe someone is wanted by his doctor, maybe there's been a death in the family, maybe someone's going free . . . . but no, things would be slower then, some one of us would be smiling. Then comes the second stage, when your entire level moves to the walls, sometimes even holding hands, a thing not usually seen. Then comes the third stage, the same two attendants each time, a nice guy and a bad guy, and they are right up to you, a smile and a frown, their big hands on your shoulders, pushing and pulling you toward the main doors. But still, and with everybody else now smiling, even your friends, you don't really believe . . . . there could have been a mistake . . . . your name does sound a little like that other guy's . . . . then comes the fourth stage, and even with your arms and legs taped to the mattress with heavy yellow tape, and even when the glue is on your head, and the wires firmly placed in the glue, and the gag stuffed in your mouth for the breaking of teeth, you say to yourself and to whatever God you can still believe in—it's not possible, it's not me, it's somebody else . . . . and in some ways you are right. . . .

We once had a Christ on our level too, before the shock room killed him. Probably some mistake was made when his commitment papers were signed because he was not like the rest of us at all. Many of us here are silent all or most of the time, never speaking or shouting and seldom moving, only working our lips or limbs or bowels when there isn't any other way out. But that's because of empty guts or minds, or because of muscles or tongues that were ripped or burned out so long ago that it doesn't even matter. But his silence was different, louder somehow, like the ending of a scream. He even looked a little like his nickname, like the man he said he was, the same thin face that was both rough and delicate, the same long hair and beard, brown I think or maybe red. And even though it was winter when he was with us, with the hall windows mostly kept open because of the stink, and with him wearing the same gray slippers and pants and shirt as the rest of us, I never once saw him shiver. Instead, his face was often shiny with sweat, as if the problem inside him was a much bigger one than any of those we were wrestling with. And I remember too that unlike any of all the rest of us, he had somehow managed over the years to keep all his teeth. But it was the eyes I remember most. On some days they were a nice blue that had in them all the hot naked lights of the ceiling, but on others they were a dark brown, like dirt is when you spit on it. I liked those sad eyes, even though I seldom had the courage to meet them directly. There was a madness in them that was so alien to what we saw in the eyes of each other that we often had to turn away whenever he got too close or even looked in our direction. That's another thing about him: he would never simply glance at anyone or anything, and even though I used to study him for the hours of many days, never once did I ever catch him staring absent-mindedly into some space of his own. Instead of merely glancing or looking at anything that had caught his attention, such as some worms in some food on a tray or a full-grown man crawling on the floor like a baby, he would get close to what he saw, not in a physical way or anything like that, but in the way that a double-barreled shotgun takes aim and gets ready and then clicks on an empty magazine. . . .

You smell the funny smell, urine and roses and rubber, you watch the crack in the wall and nothing else, you hear the

---

hushed voices, the click from the shock machine, the humming and the buzz, you see in your head a flash of diamonds when the window turns to the sun. . . .

His name was Jim Williams, I remember that now, and we were lovers. Almost everyone here who is still sane enough to move has a lover, and sometimes two or three or whatever the traffic will bear. Even now I have more than I can count since I'm the youngest by far and also the sanest, and therefore have more strength, though they are all either as hairy as apes or as ugly as sin and not very nice besides. But it was the friendship with him that was the best, a whispering on benches that has not happened since. I would get as close as I dared to tell him of the many things I had found beneath the paint with my nails. He never spoke back, but each time I mentioned something he liked he would smile, and I always tried my best to please him, sometimes even lying, telling of things I hadn't found at all. I told him all I could remember about real mother, and that I no longer minded when the other inmates called me a mother fucker, and about the second aunt and uncle and Bobby, and about real father and new mother and Idaho, and about all my homes and streets and jails . . . . everything . . . . as much as I could remember . . . . and mostly about the insanity of my tenth year that had started the whole mess . . . . and he would smile. . . .

The diamonds explode in the wet heat, your mind cracks

*open, the pain burns on for a lifetime . . . . sometimes you
come back and sometimes you don't. . . .*

. . . . And whenever he smiled, a strange feeling would
come over me; it would pound in my blood, this feeling; it
would wash over me and pound and crash all the way from
my slippered feet to my brain, and my whispers and nails
would get braver, and I would dig deeper into the benches, find
freedom there, find the courage there to help me beg, oh God,
to be a man, and even though even He had to turn away now
and then because of my bad breath, my whispers would shout
in His ears about truth and madness and fighting . . . . and
cold coffee and tea and bread and jelly, cornflakes with cute
little brown or white bugs both dead and still eating, watery
soups with strange things floating, black and brown meats that
crumble to a powder or snap like sticks, rotten potatoes and
rock-hard peas and soft sponge cake all sponged together in a
mess, a peach and almond fondue frozen nicely in a soufflé of
chartreuse custard, lemon-flavored clouds in candy-clean white
skies and mighty horses neighing trumpets of tulips and black
locomotives smoking roses as red as blood and little girls with
blood in their cheeks and blueberry-stained dresses and fat
frogs with saddles on their backs and furry honeybees with
melted sticky stingers and orange tigers in India and a desert
in Arabia with shifting sands and silver planes with wings of
lifting air and a vast and heavy emptiness that stretches all the
way in my mind from one concrete wall to the other and a

---

dream to be a king and yet another where I'm not so ashamed of being crazy anymore . . . . and even though I would never really be sure if it was Jim Williams who was smiling, or if it was Christ, or if I was only smiling to myself, I would return to the fight against madness that I had begun at the age of ten, and no matter how many times they shocked me, I would fight hard, and I would want to be a man, and I would try to forget what my arithmetic teacher had told us in my fifth grade, when she had told us that we would never change, and I would want to change, want to live, want someone else to die in my place.

7

The sun came, the sun went, father died . . . . I am ten again now in my memory and all the things and more that father had promised us when alive are now ours because of his death. Out of his grave there has come a pouring of government insurance from those who make their livings by buying death. They must have wanted him badly, having paid such a good price so quickly. Many nice things have been bought with the money. Almost all our hopes and dreams have been met with downpayments . . . . our apartment across the street from the red brick library in the green park, many new games for me to play alone, a few kind words over supper now and then with smiles, an automatic white washing machine that roars and clicks and cleans and sometimes even bangs its head against the wall, and a new clean softness about life that I had never known was possible. Even the Beverly Beauty Parlor, where new mother had before been only one of the girls as she says with a laugh, is now ours, renamed Future Beauty, in honor, she says without laughing, of the beautiful future that now lies before us. I don't know what has happened to Beverly, whoever she was. Perhaps she's dead too. Maybe that was part of the bargain. But I don't ask. I don't even care. Let them all die.

Our apartment is new and modern and clean and never before lived in, and therefore, as new mother says, without the sad memories of most houses. Everything in it, including her teakwood hope chest that no man has ever opened, is virgin and smells of new wood, fine lace, expensive perfumes, and hair lotions, and everything in our lives is now as new and as nice as her hairstyle, which is dyed a much prettier brown and piled on her head in steps. All our house is in order, carefully furnished and arranged by a worldly and impeccable taste, or so her many new lady friends keep telling her on Tuesday, which is bridge night, and each new thing has a place of its own where invisible rulers have been laid to make sure that each table leg and each end of a rug and each of everything else is never moved even one inch beyond its proper setting. I too now have my place in life for the first time, beyond which I must never go . . . . my room, the kitchen table which is also the bridge table, the bathtub and toilet and sink with my own personal towel rack, the living room with my very own chair that I must never make dirty, the school and the classrooms in it, the one long street to and from that hated school, the park that I love, and the garbage dump in the desert by the Indian shacks and the Snake River on the Oregon side of town, both of which I've been told never to go to, and where I go very seldom. And even though everything about my place in life is now normal and correct, and as orderly as the beginning of a parade, I am even more confused than ever, not unhappy really because that wouldn't be correct, but confused.

I make lists now. I don't know why I make lists, or why I make so many, I only know that I have to make them. I've even tried to list the reasons for making lists, but so far it is only an empty page with a title at the top that says—reasons for making lists, and a long white emptiness below. But I know that soon it will be as correct as all my others, and that I shall think of the reasons, or at least make them up, and then list them all in proper order below the title, either on that white empty page or in my mind or both, with the words—parade, something to do, perfection, lots of friends, proof of being alive. Or anyway, something like that.

I have lots of lists. The number of them and of things on them grow each day in piles in the closet of my room. I like that closet. I like numbers too, though not when I'm in school, and I number each list. I even have one somewhere, I don't remember where I left it since it's not in my closet, that has on it the numbers of all my lists from one all the way up to thirty-two. I think it's thirty-two anyway, the last one I did, a list of the names of all the towns around my town, but maybe it's a higher number than that. I'll either have to find it or my number list to be sure; either that or start every one of them all over again, which I don't mind doing.

I list everything . . . . the makes and colors of the cars that go whooshing by, the number of cracks counted in windows and on sidewalks, the names of trees, the different things on hats that funny-looking women wear, birds I see, insects I find, the many toys I have now that I've never had before, everything about my park that I play in and make most of my lists in, the feelings I have whenever I have them and where, and all the things of interest around and about me that I either do or do not understand that can be quickly and easily listed in small words or short sentences on papers that I hope to God no one else will ever see.

All the easy things are listed. The rest I keep in my mind. Surely, if I keep up at this rate, my collection will one day be so complete that the people in the government, or those who might want to add to their own private collections of lists, will come from all over to see me. I don't really believe that of course, and I know I wouldn't be brave enough to see them anyway, but lately it seems that almost anything is possible.

I keep only the complicated in my mind, those things that are too big to list on paper. For instance there's our new apartment and all the new things in it. Stiffly starched white lace curtains that hang smelling very nice on all the windows and never move, not even when the windows are open, which is seldom, due to the fear that new mother has of street germs. Thick pink rugs that sound beneath my feet like snow being crunched. Fat chairs with flowers and stripes of all colors that sit in every corner. Small brown tables that are shined every day with a special cloth smelling of blue flowers. A huge and expensive radio with ivory dials that sings and shouts with opera programs each evening at the end of a long blue couch that I can't sit on because I might make it dirty. Then there's the kitchen, and also the bathroom, two places I don't like at all that are filled with iron and steel and porcelain and glass and soft pot holders and softer towels and pink-flowered toilet paper on black soundless rollers and cake or hairpin boxes made of tin and bottles of perfume all the way from Paris and dozens and hundreds of hair-lotion bottles and buttons and knobs and faucets and handles and strings, all of which shine in both the kitchen and the bathroom beneath lots of long tubes of fluorescent lights that have a deadly gas in them as bright as the sun in my eyes whenever I sit either to eat or to shit.

Then there's my room . . . . a miracle that new mother gave me, a clean, quiet, and neat place where lists, dreams, and wishes are made. A black desk and chair for homework that sits between the two windows that face my park, some blue and green throw rugs that match the bed cover and the curtains, an iron plate with holes in it that is screwed to the floor so the heat can come up in winter, a cute little fan that waits for summer on the desk, a glass ash tray next to the fan should I ever decide to take up smoking, a silver nail file that is forever balanced in one of the glass grooves of the ashtray should I ever decide to give up chewing my nails, which is not likely, three green bottles of men's deodorant and one brown one of cologne nearby should I ever decide to smell better than a boy, and also a tube of white shaving stuff near the bottles should I ever feel the need to shave like a man . . . . my room, a miracle that new mother gave me, where I wake each morning with my mind sometimes singing, where I smooth and unmake every nighttime lump and fold of my new sheets and covers, where I run to my closet to look at my lists and then take off and fold and hang my new pajamas with the flower prints and the little animals and unhang and put on my new, clean, and carefully pressed clothes, and where I then wait for a while each morning . . . . usually in front of the mirror of my closet door that is exactly 51 inches and three of those little black lines on a ruler tall, just tall enough for me to see both my new sneakers and my old hair if I bend a little, and exactly 23 inches and no black lines on a ruler wide, just wide enough for me to see from shoulder to skinny shoulder if I scrunch up a bit . . . . and while standing at my mirror, and if not late for school, I list in my mind all the miracles of my room each morning, hoping each time that perhaps this time I can find a new miracle that was there all the time, but unseen up to now because I had always before stared at it too hard.

It is morning now. My east window, the one on the Connecticut side, has invited the sun to shine in my mirror. Another miracle, one that I'd never noticed before. The west window, the one on the Oregon side, is gray and dead, not worth looking at. But after school the two will change hands, and the dead window will come alive with fire and be brighter than the fluorescent lights, and it will be the turn of the morning window to die. I close my eyes and play a game. I like to pretend things; I like to play games with my mind; I like to imagine that certain things are different. I am standing now as still as a tree, listening. At first I hear nothing, except of course for the loud sounds of new mother getting breakfast ready in the kitchen, banging this pot or that pan, clicking on the stove, opening and closing the refrigerator, pouring and wiping and getting out the dishes. I use all the muscles of my body to make the tree hard, and I listen with all of me to the new sounds, to the ones I don't usually hear. Outside on the sidewalk there are people talking. I can hear tires on the street and can tell the speed and direction of the cars by listening to their motors. Several houses away there is a radio playing and some kid screaming. But all of these are old and familiar sounds and mean nothing to me, and I blank them all out, kill them and they die. The wood of the tree listens now to my room, a door moving in the draft of a window, an empty clothes hanger banging against another, a floorboard squeaking beneath my weight. I almost begin to hear the sounds that I want to hear, but then new mother coughs, and for a few seconds I can only hear that cough, and then a sigh, and her soft dress moving on her body, the fingers of her hands breaking eggshells, the gold ring on the middle finger of her left hand clicking against a knob that lights the gas of the oven . . . . and then it happens, what I wanted to happen, an explosion of sounds not usually heard, an entire new world of gold and silver sounds . . . . the growing of the tree, the noise in my head of my breathing and listening, my belt moving in and out, my toes rubbing against the cloth of my sneakers, a crack of knuckles, a flutter of an eyelid, my tongue tasting teeth, my lungs filling and hair growing, the loud blood of the tree flowing and pounding in my ears, the very center of my heartbeat, the very dead center of the world that I wish I could stay in . . . . but then new mother coughs again and I open my eyes and hear the cars on the street moving and honking again, and the people talking on the sidewalk, and the eggs and bacon cooking, and I'm back in reality again, looking around my room for new miracles. I get close to the glass of my mirror and look at my face, the only thing in my life that isn't new, so close that my breath makes gray clouds around my mouth and nose, and also around and over the dark blue eyes that I know are there even without looking at them, even without using all my courage to see me stare back, to see all the sounds and the fears and the dark and dirty secrets that others see when I don't turn quickly enough, my madness, my lists, my going to the bathroom, and also the good things that live there too, such as my new room and clothes and toys, all of which might melt if I saw them that close, like dreams in the morning, leaving nothing left but me. And when I'm done with my mirror, I breathe as I do each morning even more on my face, write with a finger my name in the cloud, leave my room, exchange good mornings with new mother, eat breakfast, brush my teeth, and go to school.

Walking to school . . . . the air is wet with mist. Bubbles of clean and cold water as tiny as anything can possibly be are hitting my face, clinging to the ends of the blue hairs of my new coat, a heavy thing with gold buttons called a pea jacket, and sliding down my schoolbooks. I stop now and then and hold the books level and the rivers stop, damming themselves into dozens of tiny pools on the shiny smooth cover of geography, forming into wide lakes on the rough fiber of arithmetic. All the world is wet today. But that's good, it is good for the air to be cleaned once in a while.

I walk through my wet park as quickly as I can without running, trying as I do each morning not to see or hear or smell anything new, saving all that for the late afternoon. Once out of my park and on the street to the school, I stop and take some of my lists out of the books and unfold them, holding them close to my body to hide them from the mist.

I've been dating them lately, not with days because I hate days, but with months, and with the numbers of the week from one to four. —September, the second week, number 84, a list of the towns around my town, I read aloud after finding the town list that I thought I'd lost. —Nampa, Weiser, Boonesville, Painestown, Idaho Falls, Clearmount, Waterton, Indian Hat, Bennington, Fruitland, Ontario, Caldwell, I read. Yes, there's lots left out. And Ontario doesn't belong there, that's in Oregon. But I'll get a map in history or geography class, finish it up good then, put them all in.

Then, as I always do, even though I'm trying hard not to notice the new things that new lists are made of, I get out a clean sheet of paper and start another. —September, the second week, number 85, a tree list, I read while writing. —Oak, beech, horse chestnut with brown ones on ground and green ones still hanging, rain dripping from leaves, elm, maple, plum, palm, bamboo, banana.

But of course I erase the last four, which in the rain isn't easy, and laugh at my joke, first making sure there isn't anyone around to hear me. Then I put all my lists back in the books and continue my walk to school. I stop laughing when I get to the playground and when all of a sudden I can't remember what it was I was laughing at. I move carefully through the crowds of kids, holding my books tight to my coat, keeping my eyes to the muddy ground, reminding myself to list later the way that a wet playground looks, but using all my strength now to look as much as possible like everybody else so I won't be noticed. I go up to the main door and stand on a step where no one else is standing, my body stiff as a tree, my arms, hands, fingers, and books like heavy wood, my eyes and mind as blank as can be, one of the ears of my head bent like radar toward the closest of the many happy voices, the other hearing again and again the first loud bell of the morning long before it actually rings.

Science class . . . . shelves and tables of glass bottle and jars holding waters, oils, and formaldehydes where tiny birds and frogs with their guts out and human babies float, some with wide mouths and some with small, and some with long glass tubes that curl in circles. Bread mold is everywhere, as are mosses, liverworts, algae, rhizomes, spores, stamens, primary and secondary tissues, abdomens, thoraxes, compound eyes, antennas, protozoas, amoebas, parameciums, flagellums, and penicillums for making roquefort cheeses. O is for oxygen, S for sulphur, Fe for iron, Sr for strontium, Co for cobalt, Y for yttrium and other rare earths; A if we've memorized all these things for a test, D if we've only memorized a few, and F when the mind remains blank, as mine usually does. Electrons, the green wings of flies, ten billion neurons in our brains, twenty million RNA molecules in each neuron, millions upon billions of different thoughts and ways to think, matter, inertia, energy, osmosis, the slight popping sound of the green head of a fly when pressed between two glass plates, the smell of yttrium and other rare earths.

I listen carefully to the teacher with my whole body, with the ends of every hair, my fingers ready, my lists ready, everything all about me ready except for my ears which are clogged, my eyes that see nothing, and the thoughts in my head that have nothing to do with the class. But I try, I swear I try, I even open my mouth so I can hear better. And I list in my mind the words the teacher is saying, but each time I think I know what he's talking about, he starts to talk about something else, and even when I go over what he's just said, and try to tie that in somehow with what he's saying now, it all becomes confused, nothing ties up with anything, and I have to start all over again.

History class . . . . a gum can passed around like an offering tray in a church. A pretty girl in a blue dress offers it to me and I shake my head and she frowns and gives it to a fat boy who drops in his gum and hands the can to another and it goes on and on. Later, and when all our school is dark and quiet, the janitor will search all the wastepaper baskets for that one can and then dig out all that gum and mash it together into one big ball and chew for hours as he sweeps, thinking of everyone but me, all those tongues and teeth chomping up and down. At least that's what I hear in the hallways.

The history teacher, Miss Collingwood, a small shadow in back of a big desk who is always unseen until she speaks, is speaking now. Her voice is as paper-thin as her body, and it comes to us in whispers of light. All the kids quiet. She is speaking to us of Huns on horseback. Her tiny hands are flying through the air as she tells us of the speed they rode, a hundred miles in one day sometimes. She tells us of the saddles they sat on, thick brown leathers and soft smelly skins. And as always she gets so caught up in her story that she becomes a living part of it, so much so that no one, not even the noisiest of us, would ever think of scraping a foot or throwing a spitball or anything. Her hands go to the front of her as if to steady the reins, her face glows with the pain of a Hun on horseback, her white arms tense as they feel for the saddle that is bouncing beneath her. —The Huns were magnificent, she tells us. —They were like animals on animals, practically welded to their small rapid horses, she says. —They rode in waves, nothing could stop them, not the Great Wall of China, not the Holy Roman Empire, not even the mighty Danube.

My class is drowned by her words. We all know that she once saw the Danube from the window of a plane some years ago, she's told us often enough. And we don't just listen to her excited whispers, we ride and whisper with her, but in total silence; we sit in brown chairs with our hands quiet on brown desks, and we are taken far away by the horses beneath us. —Mongoloid appearance, military superiority, wave upon thundering wave of fur-clad bodies on horseback ravaging and raping, she tells us. And even while I listen, with half of my mind on my problems, and the other half on the truth of what she is saying, there is a third part of me that wants so much to weld the other two together like a big ball of gum that all of me finally escapes into another world.

Over the steppes of Russia, over the Great Wall of China, splash across the Danube, up Hill 49 and into a hail of machine gun bullets. I can see wave upon wave of fur-clad bodies welded to small rapid horses. Lickity-split I am riding with my history teacher and with my huge horde of dirty stinking Huns, all of us crashing like thunder over the frozen plains toward fifty thousand waiting Chinese, give or kill a few, who will all soon be smashed into the ice and snow. We get so close that the fires of our arrows are seen burning in their slanted and evil eyes.

We smell them, their strange clothes and funny pointed hats and wooden shields made of goat skins, and they smell even worse than we do. We get so close that we can feel the frightened heat of their horses, and almost touch with our blades the cold white clouds that each red horse burns. But then, just before the kill, the slaughter, the beginning of the body count of both nations, I suddenly feel sorry for everybody and decide out of nowhere to perform yet another of my famous acts of mercy. I allow them to live. I send into the cold air my blood-curdling peace whoop and all my nation pulls to a stop, the quick hooves of our small rapid horses sliding and clawing hard in the snow. The enemy of course are very grateful, once the dust has cleared enough for them to see that this is not just one of my famous tricks, and there are smiles all around and now all of us are friends. The Chinese and their allies invite us and ours to a feast. Smoked duck and pig and goose and cat and dog. Sausages and tadpoles and squid with the ink taken out for writing, and fig newtons. Tapioca puddings with raisins and marshmallows and bright candies strung on strings for the kids, dirty little slant-eyed beasts who spit in their bowls and who throw their strings of candy into the bonfires where they pop. Football games are played with live pigs which are later burned and eaten. Squeals of delight are heard all around when huge vats of wine are opened with axes. Pea jackets are burned in jest as are hats made of bear or wolf skin and underwear made of porcupine quills. Strange music, never opera, mostly humming and drums, is played in the ears of those who have never heard nice music before. The bonfires grow larger, fed by the darkness and by the empty wine vats. Warm bodies light the night as some of the kids are thrown in too because they didn't behave. And almost everybody is having a real good time, us Huns from the frozen north with our small rapid horses, the Chinese from the warm south, the Indos from the unexplored west, the Koreans from all over the place, and nobody at all from the east because that's where the ocean is.

—What ocean, what the hell is an ocean? one of my Huns asks some Chinese guy while chewing on a leg of pig. —Vast cold waters, the Chinese guy says. —Dragons and monsters and big toothy heads with fires between teeth so hot they melt elbows and eyebrows and make ships to sink beneath waves. —I know what waves are, my Hun says after some thought. —That's when we all get up early in the morning and ride on our small rapid horses over the frozen plains and tundra, through and all the hell over everything, towns, churches, parks, little children playing in the melting snow, ravaging and raping and killing and hurting and all that. The Chinese guy smiles and picks at his smile with a golden toothpick. —Ride east, he says. —Ride east and you will be met with waves even more powerful than Huns. —That's all a bunch of small rapid horseshit and you know it, my brave Hun says before giving the Chinese guy such a whack with the leg of pig that it tears his head off and starts the war all over again.

After science, history, language, art, recess, and lunch, arithmetic, shop, geography, and gym, none of which are really worth thinking about, the four o'clock bell rings and the ears of all of us wake up as if it were morning, and the school of the dead comes alive. Our books, papers, pencils, and pens are shoved in desks, lockers, briefcases, pockets, and wastepaper baskets, and the halls that were silent and empty are filled with laughing and screaming life and then drained in seconds, silent and empty again, waiting for the janitor, and for the first bell of the next morning.

Sitting at the kitchen table . . . . new mother is serving supper, moving back and forth between the stove and our table, smiling now and then over plates of steaming food. Before me there is roast beef, mashed Idaho potatoes, green peas, milk, and red jello for dessert. My fingers search for my knife and fork. My eyes go from them to her to the food to her and to the food again. My tongue jumps in my mouth, waters and burns. I think of the school lunch, of the brown paper bag with the two sandwiches, the pickle, and the apple, all of which I chewed at, while tasting only the paper bag and while trying my best to avoid the hundreds of staring eyes, even though I knew that no one was really looking at me and in fact didn't even know I was there. My fingers pick up my knife and fork. My teeth bite so hard they almost break on the silver. Again and again, just like during the school cafeteria lunch, my eyes and throat come close to closing for good in the fear that I'm doing everything wrong. But I do it, just like at school, I pick up and eat and chew and swallow, telling myself with every heartbeat that eating is the easiest thing in the world to do, but tasting nothing. And all of me begins to go to another world, my head a block of wood that mustn't move for fear of laughter, my stomach filling with acorns, my arms and especially my hands like the stiff limbs of a tree. Every ounce of my body begs me with tight muscles to be able to jump in the food, to become a part of it and of all the other good things in life, to live, to enjoy things like others do, to be free of guilt. But somehow I keep control and cut at the meat and lift it with my fork to a small dark hole in the wood, chewing as slowly as possible, swallowing with almost no noise at all before going back to the peas which are even harder. I keep glancing at new mother, hoping beyond all other things that she won't shout or frown even though she hasn't shouted at me since father died. She smiles now, she smiles in the thin and tiny way that she always does when I'm doing something wrong. The peas fall off my fork, every single pea falls off my fork and into the potatoes. One by one they plop there like green acorns in white mud. I look up, feel the blood draining from my face, a thing I especially hate, and I feel the fear throughout my body burning my body rock-hard like petrified wood, and I tremble at the end of a fork that is just as stuck in the potatoes as I am in my chair. But she doesn't notice, or at least pretends not to. That's the way she is; instead of shouting or frowning or killing she eats her own meal, quietly and correctly, one forkful after the other, as if she's done it that way for years, knifing now and then through meat, sipping at her steaming coffee, smiling a little to herself partly because of me and also because of the opera singers who are shouting and crying at the tops of their minds in the living room. I eat faster and faster, keeping in time with the music, all the time trying my best to go slower. I keep one eye on her, on her mouth and eyes and hands, and the other on my food, trying even better than my best to not be the person I've always been, to not go any further into any other world except hers, to do everything she does and at the same time and speed. She cuts. I cut. She lifts. I lift. She puts her peas into her mouth. Mine fall all over my pants, all the hell over my world. My body turns to stone. Parts of me die. She pretends not to notice.

Walking through my park after supper . . . . things are different now. I am free of the real world, the one that makes no sense. Here there is nothing to learn, nothing to eat, no place to sit down where people can watch me. Here I am alive. My eyes, mind, ears, nose, see, thinks, listen, smells, and pay attention to every real and unreal thing that can be seen, thought of, heard with special ears, smelled, or paid an almost limitless attention to. It is getting dark now and my mind is fully awake. I am even more than alive; I am better than myself. The feet within my gray sneakers crunch and step softly on the dirt path that twists and turns around bushes, gardens with dying flowers, rocks and pebbles big and small and in the way, trees with white or dark bark, stumps that used to be trees, and one long thin parade of black ants not one of which even looked up when I stepped over. My dungarees move with my every move, tight on my legs and as much a part of me as I am of my park. My blue pea jacket and my green shirt are both too big for me, and I don't like them as much as some of my other new clothes, but they too are a part of my walk, a part of my whole life at this moment, and must be counted along with everything else.

Now and then I stop and add to my old lists or begin new ones of things I think important, things that I know I wouldn't be able to remember with just my mind. As always, even though I don't really want to, I look over my street list on one of my stops, adding to it any of the new houses that I had seen on my walks to and from school that day, their colors that I had made myself remember, anything about them that was new or un-usual, such as a big chimney or a funny leanto or a porch or a broken window or people fighting inside. Also, and I hadn't the time to stop to do this because of my being late for school this morning and late for supper this evening, I list the dogs that had run from those houses, both those I had stopped to pet and those that wouldn't let me, and the cats I had seen that I'd never seen before, and the squirrels.

A squirrel searches a branch above me, chattering and knocking down some leaves. I write—squirrel, on an empty paper, and think for a second that maybe I should give him a name, but decide not to in order to save space for more im-portant things. The falling leaves are not included either since there are far too many of them, and it would take too many hours to name each leaf. And besides, how would I remember which was which, or just who at what moment was living in a tree or rotting to death on the ground? I write—death, on my list and then erase it. I write other things down and then erase them too, as I always do when first starting out, when realizing again that the only way I can keep my lists neat is to organize everything with titles and columns, as they teach us to do at school. I write down—school, and then erase it. I carefully tear out that black smudge, clean the dirty eraser on my pants, and promise myself to concentrate on only the most important of things.

One of those is now being spurted high in the air by the finger of a little kid to my left who is trying to drink from a fountain. I start to write down—fountain and little kid, but remember again about titles and columns and instead write down—sound.

Sound. Pressure of water forced through tiny metal hole by thirsty finger. My mind records that long sentence, and my pencil writes down—water going up. The thin stream rains up and splashes down. The kid with the wet face laughs. I write down—splash, under sound, and then move on. In the distance there are cars riding on roads. Somewhere in my park there are children laughing. I write down—children, tires, horns, playing, motors, bugles, laughter. I hear birds singing. I write down—song. I hear the wind in the trees. I write down—leaves on leaves. My sneakers kick dirt, rocks, leaves, one dog mess, a piece of broken glass, a wet rag, some cigarette butts with red on the ends, and three half-rotted feathers. My mind records the names of things kicked, the number of them, what color they were or once were, and the order of them in time. I stop and close my eyes and open my mouth. I hear my papers moving in my fingers, my throat clearing, my nose sniffling, my teeth grinding and tongue moving, a plane overhead, a streetlight clicking several blocks away, a bee or something like a bee making a bee sound close to my nose, the music from a far-off radio, the distant door to the library being opened and closed, books falling on the steps, angry words, an earthquake in Peru, and the beat of my heart. . . . I open my eyes and close my mouth and move on and then stop, writing everything down as fast as I can. Somebody somewhere is running. I write down—running. I kneel like an Indian, with one hand flat on my path to feel if the earth is shaking, and when I find there's no danger of a stampede, I get up and move on. I sniff at a new smell in the air, something burning probably, but not grass or trees because then the earth would be shaking with buffalo. I stop and write down—burning, and beneath it— body sweating, bad breath, wet leaves, dog pee, brick smell from library walls, a dead-water smell from a small muddy pool in back of the library, a rotting and dying smell from a pile of garbage by the water, death, dead, useless, useless, useless. . . .

8

It would be much easier for me, for the courage I've never had, and for the sanity and the ego I now have that I didn't have then, if my memory could now say that was all there was to it, that all I did in my tenth year was to make a few lists, go through a childish phase, and that I came to the end of it and then stopped. I did stop, after a while, but that wasn't the end of it. I went through another phase, one where my hands shook too much to hold the papers. And then another, where the shaking of my hands was replaced by the unshakable fear that they would shake. And I became so afraid of that and other things that I began to push myself hard and fast into phase after phase of trying to grow up, and entered very easily into those that most children never have to go into. To pass as many of my school tests as possible with at least a D minus, and also to see my enemies, both real and imagined, before they saw me, I became an expert at staring sideways through the white corners of my eyes. And in the hallways and after school, to keep from being stared at, I often walked about with my eyes closed. And to stop the shaking, or at least to keep it under some kind of control, I held things tightly . . . . trees, bushes, railings, fences, the outsides of books, the insides of my stomach, my naked body at night, cats found, stones collected, ideas thought of whether or not they made any sense, old memories of woods and gardens, my belt, anything at all that would keep me from falling. And I began ever faster to lose hold of my mind.

A child does not crack like an old plate. He does not break quickly as an adult might, shattering all at once into so many pieces. A child is not an old plate. He is more like a new and thin cup that has not yet been filled enough to run over suddenly. He cracks slowly under the pressure; there is no hurry to it, there is nowhere to go, and not enough experience to let him know exactly what is going on when he gets there. But pain is pain, and very young children know more than we think they do. As early as the age of three I had known there was something wrong. At four and five and six I found out that that something was mostly me. And at seven or so I did somehow know that I was going a bit mad, not mad in the terms an adult would think of, insane or crazy or psychotic or anything like that, but in the quiet and special way of a baby: I was cold when I should have been warm, I was unhappy when I should have been laughing, blankets and clothes and hands and other things were hard when they should have been soft, I was often less lonely when alone, and I would stare at things that weren't there, and ignore some of the others that were, and my mind would sometimes fix on one thing for a long time and I would think very deeply to myself—my God, that isn't right.

And it wasn't, whatever it was, because nothing is ever really quite right to a child in trouble, or to an insane person, or to an adult who can still think. And it was in my tenth year that I became all three for the first time. And it was also then for the first time that I decided to fight.

I went through a phase of throwing things, mostly rocks, at cars and walls and trees, and sometimes even at certain cats I had seen do mean things to other cats. And one day after school I picked up a small rock and for no reason at all I threw it at a girl who was walking with her mother. The girl screamed, and beneath her blond pigtail a red flower I had planted began blooming. She screamed and screamed, as if she were dying, and all that her mother did was turn around and stare at me with her mouth open. People were always doing that to me when I was caught doing something wrong, staring at me in silence.

I don't remember what happened after that, but I guess I ran. I was always running in the early days of my fight, either in my mind or with my legs. Perhaps I ran to my park, that's where I went most of the time when I was afraid. There were more maple trees there than any other kind, and the wind and the squirrels, both of which were imported like me from another state, would often send the seeds of those maples spiraling toward me in the grass like broken helicopters, and I would use them to make soldiers. Hannibal and his men crossing the Alps with cold elephants. Legions of Romans marching to meet them. Hordes of rapid Huns splashing across the Danube. Nine million grown-up Russians and Germans locked

in a fierce combat along an eighteen-hundred-mile front. But
mostly Chinese and Russians, thousands of them, slant-eyed and
evil, blowing horns and bugles and crashing symbols. I would
get as excited as I dared, but except for the thundering in my
mind, I would make no sound. I would line up my armies of
maple seeds in the grass or the dirt and listen for the drums
and shouts and bugles and the rubbing of steel on leather and
the brave cries of horses. I would see tiny flags made of sticks
and leaves held up high, waving in the cold air, brown leaf
flags for one side, green for the other. Then they would attack.
Having only two hands, I could let them kill each other off
only one at a time, using a new stiff green seed to shatter an old
brittle brown one. I remember wishing I had more hands so
that I could make them all march at the same time toward a
slaughter that would kill off all the maple seeds for miles around
in one final hell. I would talk to them after the battles, when
the ground was so littered with the seeds of the maple people
who had fought my silent fight that there was nothing there
to answer back but sadness and moaning. But I would never
say anything during the battles because I always felt they had
enough on their minds with all that killing. And when it was
over, for the time being, I would even give some of the more
heroic seeds the most beautiful of funerals with kind music,
never opera, mostly humming, and with crosses white with
spit that were taken from the flag sticks and tied one on one
with blades of grass and then stuck gently over the mounds of
dirt where the broken dead were buried. During these burials

I would pretend to cry, but I would never really cry since I figured that my sudden change from general to priest would be hard enough on any remaining troops without my hurting them even more by crying like a kid. Sometimes my armies would get bored with fighting on land, as armies sometimes do, and whenever this happened, I would take them to the small muddy pool that was close to the red brick of the library wall and build them ships of leaves, big ones for one side and fast small ones for the enemy. Many a ship of war was sunk by rocks in that dark ocean, hundreds of them, perhaps even trillions, but nobody ever found out about it, or if they did they never cared enough to mention it.

I loved that library, at least the back of it. I never went inside of course; I didn't have a card. But there was a certain kind of power that I got from those bricks that helped me forget about the mysteries inside the library, the same kind of power that my sheets and covers of night would give me just before I fell in the dark sleep of my bed. A happiness of being alone, a love of my hands and body, and a kind of mental self-torture that I would enjoy for many years to come. My fingers would fight in the dirt or grass or water, or on my body at night, and I would enjoy that, but all at the same time those fingers would sometimes want to reach up and tear or pound at the brain that made them do such childish and guilty things, and I would enjoy that too. The ground would be littered with death, or the sheets around me filled with the blackest of imaginations, and my finger-generals would see what they had done and then look up at me as if to say—you're dying, why should we continue to kill and bury at the command of someone who is dying?

But generally I would win those many arguments, and my mind would keep the rest of me under control, and things wouldn't be too bad. I could feel that mind growing sometimes. I would walk down a street and feel it getting bigger and bigger, and at times the feeling would be nice, and I would continue to think my thoughts, even pushing them faster than they were already going. But at other times the feeling would not be nice, and I would know that my mind was being pushed too fast by something, and I would try my best to slow it down. But when I couldn't, when it just kept going and going with faster and more terrible thoughts, I would know that something was very wrong, and the fright would come close to blinding me; and there were many times when I would want to stop a stranger and shout to him that for God's sake something is happening to me. But I was usually able to control that too, and only did it once.

It was after school and I was listing in my mind the colors and shapes of houses on a street I had never walked before. I was making up new names for the colors I liked most, having become bored with the sounds of red and yellow and blue. I was squinting my eyes to change the houses into more interesting shapes, spitting on my fingers to wet my eyes and see things different, bright roofs curving all the way to the ground, dark windows too small to see from, steps leading only to the tops of crooked chimneys, things like that. But at the same time, as so often happened whether I wanted it to or not, some other part of my mind was running on all those questions that had troubled me during the day. Was this kid or that kid staring at me during science class? Did the teacher in history give me less homework than the other kids because she thought I was too stupid to do it, or because she felt sorry for me? Which is worse? Were those boys at the end of the hall waiting to jump me? If so, why? And isn't there any way to figure everything out all at once and grow up real quick? But no, there wasn't any way, and the questions came faster and louder, and the houses took shapes even beyond my imagination, and the colors were strange and had no names that I could think of, and I began to feel funny, sort of dizzy, and there was a noise in my head I had never heard before, like the crackling of popcorn, and a tickling deep inside, as if somehow one of my fingers had disobeyed orders and was reaching into my mind just behind my nose. And there was this man walking in front of me and I ran up to him and grabbed his arm, and I must have scared him out of his wits because when he turned around, his face had a funny shape, all lumpy and no color to it; he was as pale as a ghost, and looked a little like one of my maple seeds that I was about to tear apart. And he said something like— my God, here now, what is wrong with you, what are you doing? I had never heard anyone say that to me before, and I let go of his arm, and even though the tickling in my mind was beginning to hurt, and the crackling becoming a roar, I still somehow had just enough common sense left to whisper something to him about going to the bathroom. Then some of the horror left the man's face and without a word he pointed in the direction of my library. I guess I then probably said thanks or something; I was terribly embarrassed, and I ran as fast as I could into my park and around the library, stopping for a moment at a brick corner to look back at the man who was still standing there. Then I ran up the steps without thinking, and opened the door for the first time and went inside. Once in, everything in me began to quiet, even my heart and my breathing, and the excitement of actually being inside the red brick walls was much more than enough to make me forget my most recent embarrassment.

There was this most incredible smell of knowledge, not just of books and dust, but the actual smell of lists made by others for people to read if they had a card. It was everywhere. The quiet air was filled with it. It was fantastic. I was suddenly surrounded by more books than I had ever seen before. There were none in the apartment, except for one on how to play bridge, a couple about opera singers, and some others on how to decorate apartments. And except for the school library that I had heard about but never been to, there were no real ones, only the study kind. I walked around for a long time, sniffing the smell, trying to look as though I belonged, hoping that the librarian, sitting tiny behind a big desk piled with still more books, wouldn't notice me. It was a beautiful time. There were all these dusty little hallways, but instead of walls there were shelves and shelves of nothing but books. Great big ones, little tiny ones, and books so sucked out by minds that their bindings were falling in gray pieces to the wood floor. I read so many titles that I got a headache. And every time a real customer entered into my private world, I would obey the signs that shouted all around and walk as quietly as I could into a hallway that was empty. Just once I did reach way up to try to tap in with my fingers a skinny magazine that seemed about to fall. And that is exactly when the librarian came in to say hello and could she help me. My fingers got so startled at this that they grabbed at the magazine and it fell on my head and to the floor. I tried to pick it up, mumbling how sorry I was, but I was so scared that I couldn't get hold of it; my fingers began tearing at its cover, and I wanted to die. But instead of yelling at me or anything she smiled, saying that I was in the wrong section for children. I left the magazine where it was and got up and ran down the hall and out the door and down the steps and around the corner toward home.

I had been caught again, like that time I'd been found playing with the postcards. Someone had again entered my mind and found it to be dirty. I punished myself for letting that happen. I had gotten an erection in those hallways, though I wouldn't think about that until I got home, and for a long time after I kept my hands away from my body. I would spend hours trying my best not to think of anything at all. In the school and in my park and especially on my bed, I would sit or lie with my mind empty, and think only of things being emptied . . . toilets flushed, marble bags spilled, papers erased, onion sacks with the last onion falling out, people sick and throwing up, puddles in the sun, skies without clouds, matches blown out and cigarettes stomped, old coffee cups sitting all morning, opera turned off with a click at night, the blue eggs of robins dropping from trees to sidewalks, white bones in the desert, sleep without dreams, eyes blinded by the sun, a thick wall around me, death, blackness, nothing. . . .

But there was always something. My game would never work for very long. Only for a few minutes at a time. And then it would all be there again, all my thoughts and fears and guilts rushing in to fill a mind I could not keep empty . . . stomachs swollen, toilets and bags and sacks filled almost to bursting, huge dark animals walking in a crowded desert, a sleep almost as busy as the day, a sky heavy with clouds both day and night, my hands on my body again, millions of questions. . . .

And my mind would race all over again, just as fast as before and sometimes faster. I would think—what is wrong with me? Why does it have to be me who is so different? Why can't it be somebody else? How can I grow up real quick? How can I fight all there is in my mind that is wrong? And the questions would go on and on for hours, and be just as hard to live with as the time that was spent in trying not to question. There was no middle ground. It was either think or try not to; there was no third choice, and I always stayed me.

But I went on pushing myself hard and fast through many phases, trying to change this. I would force my mind and body to obey the wishes in the day and the dreams in the night that would come to me when the healthy part of my mind was working the hardest. And using that healthy part that I could never name or even find unless it wanted to be found, I would take a chance on each thought and dream, hoping and praying that perhaps, finally, this one or that one would work. I would go to the bathroom, after the supper or after the walking or sitting in my park, or during or after my homework, or when my busy dreams woke me with warm sweat in the middle of the night, and I would close and lock the bathroom door, sitting down and forcing my body to clean itself so hard sometimes that my arms and legs would become covered with the bumps of geese. Then I would flush, pretending it was somebody else who was doing such a dirty thing, pretending hard that all that was not flushed was clean, so clean that no one could hate me. I would wash the outside of me, scrubbing with my own personal towel my ass, hands, face, and neck until they burned red, digging in ears with fingers, and with hot water melting from the tips of those fingers all the sounds of that strange-smelling wax as yellow as pee. And with a silver clipper I would clip painfully close any toenails that had grown since last time and any of the nails of my jagged fingers that my teeth had missed, and then push my blue comb hard through my hair until my head hurt, stopping only when I would see that some of the ends of the hairs on the comb were red.

But none of these things ever worked. No matter what I did, I continued to stay me, to stay the same dirty and unlikable boy I had been for as long as I could remember. And even in the evenings after school, when I changed over and over into different clothes, blue dungarees and yellow shirt into brown dress pants and starched white shirt, smelly socks into socks smelling of soap, gray sneakers into black loafers, and dirty underwear into clean, there still wouldn't be any change, and the reflection in my room mirror would never look anything at all like my mind's picture of any of the other kids. And I would always stay me, always, even when I combed my hair differently or turned sideways in the mirror or wrinkled my mouth or squinted.

I tried lots of other things too. I even burned all my lists once, flushed the smoking ashes, made believe it was another funeral, said good-bye to the past for the thousandth time. But the past wouldn't die. And I began to make more and much stranger lists. I counted the hairs on my arm one day in the sun and ended up with the most gigantic number I had ever thought possible. I stared at the sun with wet eyes and counted and listed the colors of a prism. I listed once all the thoughts of one day from waking to sleeping, leaving out only those that were thought during breakfast or lunch or supper or in any of the classes, and on about the tenth page, it was like looking at the sun, my burning eyes wouldn't focus, the black blur of my letters meant nothing.

I watched for over an hour in my park once as a black wasp

killed and tried to carry away a heavy green caterpillar. It would lift the caterpillar in the air for an inch, then fall to the ground to scissor away the head, then lift it in the air for two inches, falling back again to cut away some fat, lifting it again to fly with it as far as four inches up and seven more toward home before getting tired and falling back again to cut and to lift, to cut and to lift, until finally the caterpillar was light enough to carry away and to eat in some private place where there were no eyes.

I took a fingerful of dirt from my park once, and on my bed I pretended I had a park all to myself and that the magnifying glass I had once bought for ten cents was an expensive microscope . . . . black and brown dirt bumps as big as boulders, silver and very rare mica bits as clear and sharp as diamonds, red bugs as small as pin points and with black legs as thick and hairy as the legs of dogs, a piece of a leaf with rushing rivers of red veins . . . . and in my park, after destroying hundreds of maple seeds with guns and bombs, I would burn leaves with the sun, holding my glass and the leaves and the roaring fires in my hands.

God came to me hard in that tenth year. He spoke to me for the first time when I was mowing an October lawn for the ten cents to buy the magnifying glass. I was running with a rusted mower and He stopped it with a rock that shot out from under the blades with such force that I was lifted into the air by the handle of the mower and thrown over it to the uncut grass in front. I had needed something, I had needed it badly, and suddenly there it was staring at me in the face, a mower on its side, a hurt stomach, my nose deep in the tall grass, my mind lifted to Heaven. We became good friends after that, and I forgave Him for coming on me so suddenly and hurting my stomach.

I went through a phase of torture . . . . brown stink bugs burned by my glass or drowned in muddy pools, black beetles smashed on sidewalks like bottles of thrown ink, the pulled-out green wings and legs of silent grasshoppers spitting tobacco juice in the dirt as dark as new mother's coffee, furry yellow bees crushed beneath shoes or rocks into small wet messes as thick and yellow as father's spit had been, and anything at all that was tiny enough to hurt.

I found a spider one day in my park and named him Roger, a Daddy-Long-Legs with legs so long they reminded me of father's. I found him with fingers and cut him with scissors, long black scissors stolen from new mother's bedroom. First I cut off the feet, and he was a Daddy-No-Feet. Then I cut off half his legs, and he was a Daddy-Short-Legs. And then I crippled him completely, and he was a Daddy-No-Legs, a soft round body sitting quiet in my hand not caring anymore. He took a long time to die.

I found a bird lying dead on the brown grass of my park one day, a robin I think because of the different color of its belly, and after examining it closely enough to make sure it was too dead to bite and not just playing a game of its own, I thought for a while on the pleasures of burying it, but then decided not to, as there were some kids playing on the swings nearby.

About an hour later I came back, having become bored with the cloud-watching on the other side of my park, first making sure that the squeaking of the swings had stopped. I bent down to look at the bird again, wanting to find out how it had died and thinking of breaking off one of the feathers to start a collection. The bird's neck had been broken. I could tell that by the way its head flopped over to one side in my fingers and by feeling the jagged ends of the bones. But instead of breaking off a feather I dropped it quickly and kneeled at a safe distance to watch. Every inch of the bird was alive. All over it there were tiny black beetles, red ants and mites, fleas and flies and other things, all of them small and busy in their jobs, wandering in and out of the feathers and the holes they had eaten. After a while I got bored and went home to eat.

That night I came back with a pack of matches. The same insects were still there, eating away and having a good time. But now there were two other kinds, huge beetles as big as two thumbs put together, one kind with a shiny black back and a yellow head, the other a dull gray but with pretty designs of orange splashed neatly all over the hard-working shoulders. They were burying the body, digging underneath and pushing and pulling. Half of the body was already buried. I pulled it out and went home to bed.

On the next day and on the next and the next, sometimes in the daylight and sometimes with my fingers lit by the stolen matches, we played this same game over and over, the beetles digging the hole deeper and then dragging the body in, I coming back to pull it out again by the tailfeathers or the feet. And each time I came back, there was more of the body sticking out. The beetles were getting tired. I was winning. I was winning. Then finally, on about the seventh day, the funeral was over, the grave was empty, the mostly-eaten corpse was resting on the edge of the hole. The burying beetles had given up and gone away to find another body in which to lay their children. I had won. But I didn't really feel good about it. They were only doing their job, playing their game, and I had driven them crazy.

I had many games that new mother had bought me when we first moved into our new apartment. One was a woodburning set. I read the directions and then used the iron woodburner to burn into the plywood the outlines of an empty rowboat in the middle of a lake filled with frogs smiling on lily pads. I thought it was a silly scene since there weren't any people, but that's what the directions said to do so I did it. Lesson number two was a bunch of Egyptian pyramids sitting in the sand. I did lesson number two but I cheated a little by making them upside down, a triangle within a triangle, a Star of David. Lesson number three was a complicated one, a south sea island or something with lots of palm trees and clouds. But still there weren't any people. Did they think I was so stupid I couldn't burn in people? Did they think I was so deaf I couldn't hear the news on the radio about people burning? I went then to my park to gather pockets of maple seeds and came home and burned them into the south sea islands and into the Egyptian sands and into the lily-pad lake. And when I got tired of that, I went back to my park to fill my fingers and pockets with grasshoppers, and for many days after until I got bored again, the stink of those burning people filled the apartment when no one was home.

Another game I had was Chinese Checkers. But I didn't know how to play the game and couldn't understand the directions. So I invented my own, thought up countless ways to move the marbles, moved those pretty glass eyes from socket to cardboard socket, pretended for many hours at a time that they could see things I couldn't. But of course most of the holes that these eyes jumped in and out of would always remain empty since there were always more of the holes than there were of the marbles. But I would try again and again to fill each hole, even though I knew it was impossible; I would work faster and faster with my fingers jumping the eyes, stopping only when my own became wet from the frustration, and when my mind couldn't take any more.

I had an erector set too. With it I would build bridges and cities, silver and shining extensions of my mind with holes in them so the wind of my breath couldn't blow them over. I didn't understand those directions either, but it didn't matter much since it was easy to fit the nuts, bolts, and girders together once I got the hang of it.

There was also a chemistry set that was filled with the magic of powders, liquids, glass bottles and tubes, and one Bunsen burner. But not even once did I ever figure out what it was that the directions in the booklet were trying so hard to tell me. So I had to make up my own magic, cheating a little with each experiment, turning yellow powder into red liquid sometimes, and then back into yellow powder again.

But the main thing about almost all these games was that sometimes the harder I played, the more I would feel the erection between my legs building hard as if in the mind of someone else's experiment. And when I would feel this happen, I would think and think and try my best to keep my hands away from my body. But when I couldn't, when my hands would just go on and on, one after the other shaking with pressures that I knew were bad, I would know that something about me was very wrong, and the fright would come close to blinding me. And even when I would try so hard with my mind that my knuckles would turn white from the grasping of the marble eyes or the glass tubes or the erector set metal, it would still sometimes be no use; I would have no control and I would have to leave my room.

I would go then to my park and gather fingers of maple seeds and as many grasshoppers as my pockets could carry. And when home again, I would throw them all into the cities and beneath the bridges and then dust them with the wet yellow powder. Then, first plucking out some of the Chinese marble eyes to watch with me, I would burn those powder-dusted backs with my Bunsen burner, or with the hot iron tip of my wood-

burning set, sitting close on the floor and watching quietly as
the grasshoppers crackled and jumped in tiny flaming explo-
sions of pain, sometimes melting to maple seeds and riding with
them like Huns all the way up through the yellow-gray smoke
of my bridges and cities. Then after a while the jumping would
stop and the fires would go out and my erection would die and
I would clean up all the blackened bodies and put my games
away.

Then suddenly, after several weeks of these games of torture,
I stopped and turned over one of a thousand new leaves, because
of God or whatever. And in desiring mercy for myself, I became merciful toward others. Instead of hurting, I began to
help. I removed flies from webs rather than wings from flies,
not the dead ones because that would be cruel to the spiders,
but those that soon would be if I didn't. I took caterpillars from
roads, ant poison from closets, and even stink bugs too from
whatever trouble they were having, but with a long stick. And
in the desert, never having seen a rabbit go up and kick another, I no longer threw rocks at rabbits.

But whatever I did or didn't do, the same fears would remain. I was afraid of things that nobody else was afraid of.
Between opera programs I would hear the war news on the
radio and I would spend hours trying to imagine men killing
men. And once on the radio I heard that sixty million buffalo,
called bison by the man on the news, had all been shot in as
little as fifty years, and I couldn't imagine that either. And I

became afraid, with a deep and uncontrollable fear that would last for years, not so much for the dead ones or for the ones who still remained to die, and not so much because I too might some-day be killed for little reason, but because I wanted so much to imagine such things but couldn't.

But of course I realize now that most of my fears were groundless, and that all of us kids stood on pretty much the same ground, and that we all shared the same fears of the same things even though we seldom shared them with each other in spoken words . . . . growing up, girls, tooth and belly aches, dentists and doctors, tests we had to pass or else death, wars on the radio that we didn't understand, slaughtered buffalo to feed dead Indians, no cards on Valentine's Day, thunder and lightning, the end of the world, death, blind-ness, meeting and talking with teachers and parents and strangers, big kids with curly hair who were smarter and tougher, the dark corners in hallways and on streets where they might be hiding, and the dark and deep inner fears . . . . am I good enough? do people like me? if I should die before I wake, where will I go? am I too tall and skinny? is my body fat and silly? are my pimples bursting? if there's a dark spot of wet on my pants will people know for an absolute fact that it came from a sink? will I burst into tears if someone hits me? are there worms in my head?

But the trouble is that all those kids, even the quietest and ugliest of them, had someone to tell about those many fears, at least as far as I know. But all I ever had was my imagination, a sick thing to begin with and not really much of a friend. I couldn't ask new mother. She had failed with father and didn't want to fail again; she would only smile at me with her nice smile and then clean the apartment again; she was too close to the perfection in her life she had always wanted. And I couldn't ask any of my teachers. They had already arrived at their perfection in life; they were there to fill heads and not to discuss the fears that young heads were filled with. And the kids wouldn't talk to me. And God as a friend was just as silent as He had been before.

There was an Indian kid in one of my classes, I don't know how he got in, and he was very dirty and quiet. His name was Leonard, and even though he was small, he had muscles like a man from working in the summer beet fields, and a face like a horse. Nobody ever talked to Leonard. But he never seemed to care much. He couldn't do anything right. And once even I made fun of him. But there was an athletic contest of some sort one day, and when he sailed over the jump bars like a gazelle, inches higher than anyone else in the history of the school, it was a whole new thing. Even Margaret Asmussen and Janet Jacobs, the two prettiest girls in the fifth grade, began to follow him around. I saw him that evening in the bathroom crying.

They taught us all in that school how to add and substract, and later, how to multiply. They taught us about amoebas and parameciums, and about yttrium and other rare earths, and how to make neat columns for our lists, and how we could recognize each and every twist and turn in the Lo Lo Trail, should we ever have the chance to come on one. And we all had to memorize to a mindless perfection the name of each Idaho county from the Sawtooth Mountains to the Bitterroot, and that Tegucigalpa is the capital of Honduras, and that the quality of mercy is not strained, and that Julius Caesar was born on the twelfth of July. And while sitting quiet at brown desks on small rapid horses, we all learned how to cross over the Great Wall of China, how to enter into the Holy Roman Empire, and how easy it is to splash across the Danube. But they didn't teach us how to cry. We had to learn that by ourselves.

9

—Go ahead and cry if you want to, the principal of my school said to me one morning in the last week of October. —Go ahead, cry all you want, we understand.

But I didn't. I put my hands deep in my pockets to stop the shaking and tried my best to look as normal as possible. At my feet a dark shadow from the light above me carried my head in four directions. Through the open door in back of me I could hear a classroom of kids pledging allegiance to a flag. On one side of me a windstorm was shouting at the windows. On my other there were four ladies I had never seen before; they were sitting in a row facing me, smiling sadly, shaking their heads and making small noises with their tongues each time I glanced their way. Someone began running down the hall and the door in back of me was closed, shutting out the footsteps and voices of kids. The principal, who had called me to his office to tell me I had just been adopted, was sitting in front of me with his fat red face propped up on his desk by the same huge and painful fists that had threatened to beat me with a wooden paddle several times in the past month because of my poor grades. —Go ahead and cry, he kept saying. I began to hear again the loud whacking sounds, and the cries of the kids being spanked. —Please, sir, I thought of saying. —Please, sir, I won't do it again. But whatever it was I had done, or had not done, was not now in question. I stared down at my four shadows and then at the windows that were now being drenched with rain.

—Everything's going to be all right from now on, I heard one of the ladies say. —You've been through a lot, so many different houses, but now we've found you a real home, I heard another say.

I began staring at the principal's mouth and fists. Again and again he was telling me to go ahead and cry if I wanted, with every one of those ladies shaking their heads faster and clucking louder each time. He was begging me, they were all begging me to cry, to do the correct thing, to act normal in front of the adults. But I didn't.

So that was that. I had wondered why it was that new mother hadn't dressed in her white uniform that morning. And now I knew. There were certain ladies in our town, perhaps the four in the principal's office, whose hair would have to be dressed some other day. New mother had taken the day off to pack my clothes and games and sign some papers. But there was no use in my getting upset about it. It was just another phase in my life, just another someone either coming or going away. The door in back of me opened and I could hear the scraping of chairs. I was turned around gently by the ladies, who were the officers in new mother's Eastern Star, and walked into the hall where I was introduced to my two new parents. As the three of us left the school to walk into the rain, I could hear singing from some of the classes. Then I sat between them in the front seat of their car and the door of the old Chevy shut and I was off again.

All the way across town and into the desert toward my new house, past the cemetery and the garbage dump and the Indian shacks, my new parents talked to me about what good friends we were going to be as soon as we all got to know each other. I smiled and nodded back each time they said something or patted my knee or gave me a hug, and each time I did this they seemed even more happy with their choice of an adopted son, and even less aware of the fact that I wasn't talking back.

The old Chevy stopped. He got out. She got out. Hands reached in to help me and I banged my head slightly on the door. When the dizziness went away, I was standing on desert sand in front of my new house. There was no sound for a while. Even the wind, which I would later grow to hate, was dead.

Even the rain had stopped. Long silent drops were falling from the eaves of the high black roof, making a deep row of holes in the sand on both sides of the wooden steps. We stood close to the car for a while without moving, as if we had come to the wrong place. But no, it was the right place. The faces of my new parents were happier than I had ever seen faces before. But it was all so confusing. Were they making fun of me? Were they laughing at me because they could see the numbness in my mind? Did they think it was funny that I understood absolutely nothing of what was going on?

But no, it wasn't that, there was some other reason. A hand touched my shoulder. On my other side there was another hand playing with and pulling on my elbow. And then, when I leaned backward and put the brakes on both shoes, they laughed out loud for the first time, and all of a sudden I could hear the raindrops splashing in the hundreds of tiny puddles. And they laughed again when my legs insisted upon moving slowly, and began to chatter in what I thought at first was a foreign language. But all these were happy sounds, just like in the car. And as numb and confused as I was, I did my best to force every muscle in my body to listen, and I began to hear some of the words. They were saying the word wonderful over and over. But it was me. It was I who was wonderful. And I heard raindrops crashing loud as footsteps, and was not so frightened anymore.

—Wonderful, wonderful. After all these years of trying to adopt, we finally have a son. My God, we actually have a son. . . .

And then we went up the noisy steps and into the darkness of the house. But as soon as the door closed and the lights were turned on, my ears plugged up again, my eyes opened wide, and my mind stopped working.

10

The house my memory now lives in is much bigger and older than anything I had ever lived in before. It stands deep in the brown empty desert, about a mile away from the green, oasis-like town that is now turning red and gold in the autumn of my memory, and about half that distance from the town's garbage dump where the Indians of the valley live in shacks. All the valley is surrounded for miles around by hundreds of brown foothills that a million years ago had been green, a small part of a shining prehistoric lake called Bonneville. Blowing over these hills almost every day, there is a special wind from the east called The Wanderer by the Indians. It is this wind that does the most damage to the Indian shacks and that blows the hardest against my house, often knocking down the foot-long black shingles and planting them like a garden deep in the sand by the gray basement windows. The Indian shacks have gardens around them too, but theirs are filled with many colors, bits and pieces of the garbage dump carried back by the brown children or blown to their sand by the same wind. Like those shacks, but quite unlike the nice clean apartment from where I had just been moved, my new house is always dark, and there is dirt and dust on everything.

It had begun as a hotel during the Snake River Gold Rush at the beginning of the century. When the gold gave out, it was abandoned and the second floor had never been finished; there were about ten rooms up there I guess, but the skeleton beams of their walls served no other purpose than to support the huge black roof. I never went up there, except sometimes in my mind. The wind did though. I often listened to it at night, along with the mice, as it blew around and through those bony rooms, and there were many hours when it seemed to be trying hard to blow down the rest of the house.

But of course it was the first floor that I knew best, and it was there that I began to make lists again, though only in my mind because of the fear I had that someone might read them and send me away again. Except for the large bathroom and the gigantic kitchen with the iron stove, almost every room had at least one or two glass bookcases, each ornately carved and towering above my head. And behind those glass doors that had been locked for so many years that the holes in the locks were filled with rust, there were few books, but lots of other things, collections mostly, bits and pieces of the desert that had been picked up and caged a great many years ago. Rocks mostly, hundreds of them of all sizes and shapes, lying in neat rows on the dusty shelves. And dozens of arrow and spear heads of black flint or red obsidian, some as sharp and tiny as a fingernail, others as big as the rocks, and each finely chiseled to a deadly sharpness. And many small stones that had in them the white fossils of bones or shells of tiny animals that had lived on the valley floor when the desert was a shining lake. Each item in every collection had attached to it a yellowed piece of paper giving the date and place it was found, but because of the age and dust none of these were readable. There were also many old bottles, most of them red and green and yellow, each filled with a piece of sagebrush or some other dead plant of the desert. And there were photographs, some framed in wood, some in silver. The photographs were all yellowish-brown and the people in them were dressed in strange clothes, and no one was smiling.

There were other unsmiling things in that house, lots of others, not even counting the people. Standing next to one of the glass cases there was a wooden Indian who had once sold cigars. He was about five feet tall, and he wore red and blue wooden feathers down his back; the fist he held out was filled with dust, broken fingers, and sharp wires. By another glass case there was a giant brown spinning wheel, spinning long gray cobwebs. And in a dark corner of a large living room of ancient dusty furniture, there was a cactus a little taller than me that had been found many miles to the south. It was brown and hard, the home of many insects, some of which made tiny buzzing sounds, as if they were sawing on something.

Dead, stuffed animals were everywhere, inside or on top of every glass case, hung on the brown or yellow walls of almost every room, sitting and staring at me from the darkness of many corners, and they were the one collection that I hated a thousand times more than anything else. They were desert animals, caught, killed, and beheaded in the desert a very long time before. The heads on the walls were mostly deer. And everywhere else there were smaller animals that had been stuffed whole, chipmunks and snakes and birds, and others that I didn't know the names of. But mostly there were rabbits, jackrabbits I guess, each sitting or standing in a different position, some with their paws in the air, others crouched low, as if still waiting for that bullet. Most of them were brown or white, and every one of them wore the same blue marble eyes that someone had lovingly placed in the dead holes a long time ago.

I spent hours staring at the antlers of the deer, trying to imagine the bodies that had once been beneath those heads, great swift bodies running, pawing at the naked sand or in the cold desert snow, standing quick with their white tails at attention at the slightest sound, then running again before the howling of dogs and the shouts of the hunters. I often wondered, was it winter when they were shot? It got very cold in the winter there, and perhaps they were glad to be out of it. I listened sometimes, scrunched up as small as I could on the floor or in a chair, listening. At first, when I did this, my ears wouldn't work, only my eyes. But if I stared long and hard enough, watching the white breath of those deer pouring out in the snow, my ears would begin to work, and I would hear the breathing, the gunblasts, the growling teeth of the dogs.

And I would feel the warmness of the blood pouring out in the snow, and see and hear and feel the long thin legs kicking as the hunters homed in crying—good dog, good dog, watch out for those feet. And then BANG! It was all over except for the cutting, and the patting of the animals' heads.

All the deer had bright red marbles shoved in the holes of their eyes, unlike the dull blue ones of the rabbits. All the rabbits were small, like children, unlike the deer who were as big as the adults who had killed them. The chipmunks, birds, and snakes had no marbles to see with. They stared at me and at one another with dark, vacant holes. I did not like to look at them.

I was kept home from school all the days of my first week, and mostly what I remember from it is the constant chatter of my new parents. All day long, every day of that first week, they stayed home from their jobs to be with me and they talked and talked and talked, but I heard almost nothing. I would walk around their big house from room to dirty room, my ears filled with the most unbelievable of sounds, my eyes staring at things I had never seen before, and never once did I ever even come close to understanding the words or the sights or the reasons for my still being alive. I had never heard such words before, not spoken to me, and I had never seen so much dirt and death collected together all in one place. Even the flies were dead. Brown, curled streamers of flypaper hung from each ceiling, and whenever I reached up to hit one, the dead flies would seem to come alive again, jumping off and falling slowly to the floor. Each time I did this my new parents would laugh, saying that even these were part of their collections.

My bedroom was at the back of the house, and in it was the collection that had done most of the killing. On one wall, next to a glass case filled with rocks and close to my antique brass bed, there were about a dozen old rifles and shotguns held up by wooden arms and locked tight by rusty padlocks as big as my fists. I was scared of these too, but each time I showed fear, at least for that first week, my new parents laughed, and told me there was nothing to be afraid of.

I was surrounded now by the pain of other things, and by fears much darker than I was used to, many of them wearing little yellow papers that I couldn't read. I had long ago glued a label to myself, as the rocks and arrowheads had labels; but unlike those collections living dead behind cold glass, my face and the label pasted across it were quite readable, or at least so I thought, and in spite of my numbness I was very surprised when it took a whole week for my new parents to see my madness.

—Come, look at our stuffed animals, they would say, pulling gently on my arm. —And look at all the fossils we found out in the desert; they were under a great pressure for thousands of years, and that could mean oil around here, you know. —Come, have dinner with us, we'll teach you how to set the table. —Come into the living room and talk to us, you're such a quiet boy, tell us about your past, tell us how we can make you happy, let us know whenever you need spending money for the school lunch, for candy and soda pop, for games and toys, for new clothes and shoes, for anything that might make you smile and be happy and talk to us. —Come, sit close to us, it was your long fingers we noticed first, we sat in on several of your classes, don't you remember, you glanced up at us several times, wondering who we were, and it was your fingers that made us decide to adopt you, they are long and slender like those of an artist. —Come, sit close to us, let us tuck you in at night, let us love you, for we've always wanted a son. . . .

And, oh God, above all other things in my life I wanted to be tucked in at night; I wanted to be able to look through their eyes and see as they saw the only three things of their life that they loved . . . . each other, the ten-year-old boy they were so lucky to own after so many years of trying to adopt somebody, and the rocks and stuffed heads and bodies of their beloved animals. And I wanted so much to have breakfast and dinner with them at their great wooden table without my hands shaking, and to tell them about my past without my throat choking closed, and to talk to them about a thousand things and to ask a million questions. And above all else I wanted terribly to hide my fear and hatred of their dark and dirty house and to let them know how much I loved them. But I never did any of these things. I knew from past experience it was all hopeless. And I knew that they too would someday leave me, and that there was nothing I could do about that or about anything else.

Even now, I can feel the gentleness of that first important day, the arms surrounding me and the hands touching, the promises whispered by kind voices soft in ears that had never heard such sounds before. But I never once spoke back. I couldn't. My mind and body were too numb. I guess at the beginning they thought my silence came from nervousness or shyness or something, and that it would pass as soon as I got settled into my new life. But after a week or so had gone by without my ever once saying anything, except of course for good morning, good-bye, and could I have another glass of milk please, they finally began to realize I would never talk to them, and they then stopped talking to me.

But it was not anybody's fault really that the adoption didn't work. They were not to blame for all the unhappiness that would live and grow in the darkness of that mad house for the two months I would stay there, any more than I was to blame for what happened to me there, for all the painful madness that would remain with me even long after I had left that house, for years in fact, as if my pockets could never be emptied of the sharp wooden splinters of the beams of that house that I sometimes collected. The blame goes nowhere. There were too many people. Too many years. And most of all, too much loneliness, the almost unbearable silence of all my previous years that had turned me silent now. And it was with this final family of my life that all those years caught up with me, and it was my turn now to make others lonely. And it was in this house that the madness finally took over, and here that my long journey through institution after institution was begun.

My new parents didn't stop loving each other because of me and my silence, but they began to think of me as just one more disappointment in a life filled with things not going right, just one more small and almost invisible part of a large house we all hated, something not quite human at times that moved and made strange noises in the darkness and did dark things. And because of me, they went back to where they had been before, to that darkness, and they stopped talking even to each other, started drinking again, and once again stopped loving life. I am sorry for this; I have been sorry for a great many years, but there was nothing I could do. I had my own problems. I was ten years old.

There was a very old woman who lived with us, the mother of my new father I think, and I guess it must have been during that first friendly week that I met her, though I don't remember ever seeing her for a first time. It was she who had found, shot, stuffed, and labeled all those parts of the desert when she was very young, and she looked in some ways like one of her animals, sad and gray and never moving. Her room was the biggest in the house. One wall was not a wall at all, but a fireplace of red bricks that covered that entire side of the room all the way up to the high yellow ceiling. There were more of the glass cases and animals in that room than in any of the others. The deer heads on the walls had much longer antlers than those anywhere else in the house. And even the dozens of stuffed rabbits seemed bigger and sadder there. But because of the old woman, and because my new parents seldom came into her room except to move or feed her or help her with the bedpan, I began to spend all my time there after school.

At night she slept on a brass four-poster bed that, except for the fireplace, was the largest thing in a house filled with large things. On the wall over her bed there were dozens of old photographs framed in silver, most of them of the same young girl at different ages doing different things. In one picture she was riding a funny-looking bicycle with big wheels down a desert road. In another she was looking scared on a horse. And in those that were closest to the ceiling, so far up that I'm sure she could no longer see them, she was grown up, quite beautiful, and always wearing or carrying different guns.

But by the time I had moved into her house she was no longer young; the girl and the young woman had become an old woman who sat humming all day in a wooden wheelchair made of wagon wheels and soft blue cushions. Years before something had crippled her spine, I don't know what, maybe a horse or sickness, and she could no longer speak or move, and had to be carried by her son each morning and night from one resting place to the other. Her thin and slightly bent body was always kept covered by piles of soft shawls and blankets of many colors, and I never once got to see that body, even though I was always curious about how such an old and bent body might look. When she used her bedpan, with her son's help, I was always asked to leave the room, and as far as I knew, she never bathed.

Her face was tiny and wrinkled, all nose and chin, and both were as sharp as any of the beaks of her stuffed birds. The space between the two was just barely enough for my new parents to fit food through. Her chin, the end of it white with short curly hairs, was forever streaked yellow from the eggs, bananas, and oriental tea, the only foods I ever saw her eat or drink. The top of her bird-like head was white too, but only in splotches; the many bald spots were dark with blood, much darker even than her tiny hands, which were red and bony, like claws. It was her hands that first drew me to her, her wonderful hands that made me love her; except for her yellow eyes and thin red mouth and what she did in the bedpans, they were the only parts of her that moved. They were always doing something, those hands, they were forever moving about, scratching at the well-worn arms of her wheelchair, fussing at her many shawls and blankets, or dancing on the thick cloth of her knees. Only at night would they sleep.

There was one night in that first week that I remember better than the others. I was sitting in pajamas next to the old woman's wheelchair and staring into the fire. There was no sound for a while, but the more I stared at the flames, the more I began to hear again in my mind the sounds I loved so much. It was the music that my history teacher often played for us on her record player while telling us of the great battles of history.

The principal did not approve of that record player at all, and had come into our class several times in the past month to tell her to turn it off. But it was mostly because of the forbidden music that we loved that class, learning more there than in any of our others. And while listening again to that beautiful music, I began to see in the flames the men of my favorite lesson. And it was then, I think, that my fingers first began to run on the thin brown rug like Huns, and to climb up the thick brown spokes of the wheelchair like Huns. For this was forbidden too, just like the music. It was wrong to let my feelings go, and at the age of ten, play like a small child.

And then I began to hear the voices of my new parents who were in the next room. But their voices were not happy. There was no longer any laughter. The word wonderful was not being used. And I played as fast as I could, at the same time forcing my entire body to listen. And after a long time of trying, there was a popping noise in my head, and both my nose and ears unplugged at the same time, and the music instantly stopped as if the principal had just come in. I could hear the crackling of the flames now, and the humming of the old woman, and I could smell the urine smell of her body. But there were other sounds too. —Poor mama, poor mama, I could hear my new parents saying. And then terrible sounds. —Why is he acting so strange? Why doesn't he speak? What kind of child is that? Is he crazy?

It was somewhere near the end of my first week that I slowly began to come out of the shock of being so suddenly surrounded by so many strange things. Then Halloween came. My new parents by then had given up on me and returned to their night jobs, he on the railroad and she as a telephone operator. The old woman was humming quietly in front of the fire I had just built.

I found a large brown paper bag behind the noisy refrigerator. Then, wearing the same face and clothes I wore every day, I walked down the long dirt road past the garbage dump, the Indian shacks, and the cemetery, and into the town to begin knocking at doors. On my first few stops I got the usual treats: jelly beans, candy corn, apples, and pennies. But on about my fourth block, when my bag was already heavy, I knocked on a door that opened and closed before I could say a word. My bag dropped to the cement steps. I took out the brick they had given me, threw it to the lawn, and walked down the street for many blocks without stopping, trying to get my ears to forget the laughter, never once even coming close to understanding why those people had done such a thing.

It must have been about an hour later, and when my bag was so heavy with real treats it was dragging behind me on the sidewalk, that I looked up to find myself suddenly surrounded by a large group of boys of all ages. There were dozens of them, all banded together in the dark wearing black masks and strange costumes. There were witches with black gowns and old brooms, pirates with wooden swords and skulls and crossbones painted white on pointed hats, kangaroos with candy-bulging front pockets, Indians with war bonnets of plastic feathers, clowns with baggy clothes and painted faces, soldiers with rifles, police with clubs, many rabbits and bears, and one big retarded kid from the eighth grade who didn't need a mask or costume because of his funny face. And I was accepted by them, this was the main thing, some of the kids were actually talking to me; and I became so drunk with happiness that I instantly gave away more than half of the contents of my bag to three of the smaller kids who had just started out.

At first we all walked slowly in the magical darkness, talking in hushed voices, crossing the street quietly at each house to go to the house opposite, then crossing again, demanding at each door the treats that none of the other days of the year had given us. But then, after many peaceful blocks, things began to change, and our dozens grew into a hundred or more, and with each block we walked, our costumes became wilder and our voices louder, until in time it seemed that every boy in town was with us. Then something very different happened; one of the little kids began screaming that he'd been poisoned. Instantly, or at least as quick as it takes a hundred happy children to turn into an angry mob, we left that kid sitting on the curb, choking and throwing up in the gutter, and we left the few girls and mothers who were with us, and we began running through the streets, all of us yelling as loud as we could, tearing off our costumes and masks, taking handfuls of treats from our bags to throw back at the doors and windows we passed. We went crazy; we ran into one yard and tore down a clothesline and tied it around the house and laughed at the frightened faces of the adults in the windows; we broke windows at another house, and threw rocks at streetlights; we barricaded one street with logs, doll carriages, broken bicycles, and little kids, and when we heard the sirens screaming at us we all charged past the library of my park and got comfortable behind the statues and bushes, waiting, breathing, and coughing as quietly as we could. Then when the cops came, we all rose up screaming again, and threw rocks, wooden rifles, and old brooms toward the flashing red lights and at the angry voices of the adults. It was then that the real crazy things began to happen.

Some kid was caught, and we all became quiet again, listening to the horrible screams of that kid who sounded as if he were being beaten to death by the cops. Then we began running again, but quietly now and for many blocks, past the firehouse, the post office, and the school, the screams of that kid staying with us for a long time, our imaginations running with us all the way to the cemetery at the edge of town where the desert began.

We entered the cemetery slowly, catching our breath, wanting to be scared, wanting things that I didn't understand. I sat down on the half-dirt and half-sand ground of that dead place that divided the town from the desert, and in the light of the bright moon that hung far over the desert, I watched with some of the other young kids who were still with us, as the older ones walked among the gravestones, each yelling out when he found a stone with his name on it.

—Here it is, a kid would shout when he found the name of some long-dead relative. Then he would pee on the grave and we all would laugh, or he would pull up from the ground the plastic flowers, or the metal spikes planted by the various clubs, and threw them toward the dark trees of the town.

—Here's mine, another would shout, getting his friends to help him push and pull until the gray stone toppled over.

Several stones went down this way; one thin one that nobody seemed to belong to even broke in half, and for a while we were happy again. But then the craziest thing of all happened. That big retarded kid from the eighth grade sat down on the stone that had broken and began howling at the sky, the enormous white lips of his funny face wide open, as if he were trying to swallow the moon. Then the sirens in town began screaming at us again, and we forgot about him, and for a few minutes there was talk of running to the Indian shacks a half-mile away, of bundling up sticks of sagebrush to make torches, and of burning all those shacks to the sand, a thing we felt sure the police wouldn't mind. But they were too far away, and we were all too tired, and the sirens were getting louder.

All the other kids split into small groups and began to walk back in different directions toward town. I left my bag in the sand and went the other way, down the long dirt road past the Indian shacks and the garbage dump toward home, and collapsed in bed, not even dreaming of my last memory of that night, of that big retarded kid from the eighth grade, who as far as I know is still sitting there howling at the moon.

It was some time after Halloween that the air raid–fire drills were begun by our town because of the war in the Far East that we then seemed to be losing. We would all be sitting at our desks, doing tests or painting pictures or something, and then suddenly we would begin to hear a moaning sound so low and strange at first that it would seem to be coming from all the walls around us. Then it would build, and our heads would all rise up one by one, like those in a herd of deer that had just heard a hunter step on a twig. And the dogs of the town, expecting the high-pitched scream of the tall yellow siren on top of City Hall that had hurt their ears before, would begin the barking and the howling that only for a while would drown out that terrible sound. Then it would come, and no one would be able to hear the dogs, and the kids and the teachers would all jump soundlessly from chairs and desks and crawl and hide beneath them like dogs under perches. There we would stay for a long time with our blood pounding in our ears, and with our imaginations listening very close as every single plane in China attacked our desert Idaho town, dropping bombs and setting fire to our homes, destroying everything. But there were some sounds, at least in my ears, that were even worse than this: down the hall I would hear some of the kids from the lower classes, those from the second and first grades mostly, crying and calling out for parents that by now were probably burnt to a crisp. And then, after a few seconds of strange silence when we would hear only the dogs and the littlest of kids, the All Clear would sound, and that siren would die lower and lower until dead, and all over town we would hear the dogs barking and howling again, and it would be a very good sound.

We would all get up then, and line up, and walk on shaky

legs in orderly lines to the play-yard, where for a long while we would stand and hear a speech from our principal on the evils of Communism. And when it was over, we would pledge allegiance to a flag that was blowing in the wind, and sing the national anthem as loud as we could, and then go back to our classes.

Our school was slightly higher in elevation than the rest of the town, and while we stood listening to the speeches, pledging allegiance to our flag, and singing at the blue empty skies, we would be able to see the smoke rising from the parks and the empty lots where the bonfires had been lit all over town by the Civil Defense. Our teachers were mostly quiet during all of this, except for one fat woman from the third grade who had tears falling down her face all the way up to and sometimes beyond the dogs barking again. I'll never forget her face, or the faces of some of the smallest kids. They, like me, were frightened half to death by the whole thing, most of us too scared even for tears. And I remember that I always felt, even though I never talked about it with anybody, that like me they too could smell the stink of the rising smoke, and could see the trees and houses of our town burning, the hot red flames of Communism licking at the most civilized parts of our desert oasis, and could hear the roar of the motors as the planes flew back to China, the dirty stinking yellow men in them laughing happily at having hurt so many children.

It was my history class, and that class only, that meant anything at all to me in school. I liked my history teacher, Miss

Collingwood, very much, partly because she, that small and paper-thin woman who had been so nice to me on my first day, was the only one in that school who ever seemed to notice I was there. But mostly because of the things she taught, and the way she breathed life into every lesson, sometimes even bringing her record player to school even though we all knew that the principal did not approve of such things. But for some reason that I have never figured out, I was constantly mixing up all those lessons, no matter how nice the music was, never being even a little able to separate any one of them from each other.

For instance, there were all those Huns on small rapid horses that I greatly admired for the way they had crossed so easily over the Great Wall, had entered so easily into Rome, and had conquered most of Europe by merely splashing across a river. And then, all mixed up in my mind with those beloved animals on top of animals, there was some Greek place called Thermopylae where the arrows of the East were so thick in the air that they hid the Western sun, and where the commander of the defenders had said simply—very well then, we shall fight in the shade. And also, and among many others, there was a man called Horatius by his close friends, a big and brave man with bulging muscles who once stood in the middle of a little wooden bridge and shouted to himself and to all who had ears to hear with—this is it, I go no farther, I shall stand and fight here until death. And then, but quite different from all those other things in history, there was the burning of a library in a town called Alexandria, the most horrible thing that man has ever done, or so my history teacher kept reminding us. But I could never figure out just who it was who had lit the matches; was it my Huns, the Romans, who? And lastly, there was somebody in history who arrived at some place, took it immediately, and sent back by messenger only three words—Veni, Vidi, Vici. I arrived at this God-forsaken place, I saw the worst nightmares that can be imagined, and I conquered them at once.

But the main thing in my mind about all these lessons was that each had a lot to do with bravery, something that I lacked more than any other thing. And even though I could never separate A.D. from B.C. or good guys from bad or just who had done what and why, I was fascinated by the fact that certain people could win over others, and all so easily, even if only on a printed page, and even if by winning they had to burn pages. How brave it is to burn a library and horrify a history teacher, how brave it is to try to defend all those lists and books even when you know it is hopeless, or to cross the Alps with cold and protesting elephants, or to try to defend a river or a wall or a golden city, or an important patch of cold ground that is darkened by a sun covered and knocked out of the sky with arrows where the commander of the defending troops can still so calmly say—very well then, we shall fight in the shade.

And because I could never tell the difference between one thing in history and another, I had to invent a plan that would take care of the problem. I had to do what an algebra teacher would teach us to do many grades and years later, though of course in my fifth grade there was no name to it; I found what for me at the time was the lowest common denominator and I made my mind in that fifth grade think only about Huns. Thereafter, no matter what was taught in that history class, I pretended that Huns were always somehow involved. Even when the Spanish Armada set sail and sank, I saw only my Huns, dirty and crouched low in their boats made of leaves. But this plan too, like so many of my others, became almost uselessly complicated when I learned there were different kinds of them, that there were also nations called Tartars, Turks, White Huns, Magyars, Mongols, Goths, and Visigoths. But anyway, for me in that fifth grade and for many grades after, everything in history had something to do with Huns, everything, even that frightening war in the Far East.

But enough of that. It was the old woman who meant the most to me in the winter of my tenth year. In the cold mornings my dreams would leave me and I would wake and dress and look at myself for a while in a small silvery mirror that hung on the wall close to the hated gunrack, and tilted downward a little to show everything about me but my feet and face. Then, first looking over my games, toys, and lists that my new parents had piled in one dusty corner and that I no longer played with, I would go into and through the long dark hall to the great wooden table in the dining room and sit in a chair that was closest to the heat of the big iron stove in the nearby kitchen. There, first saying a silent good morning to the wooden Indian, I would eat my cereal or eggs and bacon while listening

to the sawing of the insects from the cactus, and the humming
from the old woman who was being fed her eggs and tea two
rooms away, and then say good-bye to my unhappy new parents
whose eyes, along with those of the animals, I would feel staring
at me all the way up to the time I walked out the front door.
Then I would walk the long dirt road past the garbage dump
and the Indian shacks into town and to my school, where I
would learn nothing. During the school lunchtime I would
sometimes go to my park, always being careful not to get too
close to new mother's apartment house since I might forget I
no longer lived there and go inside, and that would be very
embarrassing. But because of the long walk, and the air that
was getting colder each week, and the absence of both the insects and my desire to kill maple seeds, the visits to my park
became fewer and fewer each week. And in the cold evenings
when school was over, I would walk the dirt road again and
go home, going instantly to the old woman's room where my
day would really begin.

I don't know when it was that I first fell in love with the
old woman, or exactly why it was that this happened. Perhaps
it was in my second week, when most of my numbness had
worn off, and because she was the only person in my life who
had ever had a good reason for not talking to me. Or perhaps
it was in my third week, or my fourth, and the reasons for my
deep feelings were too many to count either then or now. But
I do remember that mostly it was her hands that drew me to

her, her hands that made me somehow feel I was human and not so alone in this world as I had thought.

On most of these evenings I would first remake the dying fire that her son had made in the mornings, my fingers and arms often aching from all the heavy logs I would carry in from the woodpile on the back porch. Then I would sit and become comfortable on the thin brown rug by her feet beside the round wagon wheels of her chair, always on the right side for some reason. And together for hours we would watch the fire, the only sounds being the crackling of the logs, the whisper of the busy feet of the mice on the second floor and inside the four walls of our room, the sawing buzz of the insects from the cactus in the dining room two doors away that I think now were probably termites, and the constant humming from the old woman's mouth.

There were several miracles that would happen each night as I sat there, sometimes not moving except to get rid of the cramps in my legs once in a while, and except of course for my eyes and hands, and my ears too, if ears can be said to move. Not real miracles or anything like that, but very small and nice things that I would like to think of as miracles.

Hours and hours and hours would pass while I sat by the old woman's feet, and in time I would begin to see strange things in the fire I had built, and in the old woman's eyes, and on the walls where the animals stared at us with their red or blue marbles or dark vacant holes. The old woman, in spite of the people who considered her stone deaf, and contrary to what they thought about the deadness of her mind, was in fact quite able to hear and think, and was almost as shy as me.

I learned this by watching her hands, moving as they had moved for years, walking on long bony fingers through her shawls and blankets, crawling along the wooden arms of her chair, or resting nervously on the softly blanketed place of her knees. And my own hands, becoming braver with each week, and not so frightened anymore by all the eyes that I knew couldn't really see me, would begin their own walking, slowly and on tender fingers at first as if they were afraid of breaking something and of being laughed at, then stronger and more courageous with each fire-bright night. No longer were my hands so concerned with that dirty place between my legs. My hands no longer even shook, except of course when in school; at night they were as brave as Huns, careful in the firelight and slow as shadows at first, then quick and strong like men on horses, magnificent men riding over the brown rug, climbing in and out of the brown wooden spokes of the wheelchair, teasing sometimes over the tiny green-slippered feet that never moved, or flying like silver metal planes through a warm air filled with the humming, buzzing, and crackling of our wonderful room. There was life to my hands and fingers now, unlike the times in my park when there was always the fear of being caught, and there was happiness in my mind. I was no longer afraid. I was no longer afraid.

Even more miraculous than my lack of fear, my sudden

freedom, the splendid knowledge that now finally I could play the way I wanted without my eyes and ears forever worrying about some sudden discovery by some stupid kid or gardener in a park, or by a new mother who might come home unexpectedly and hate me even more than was necessary, there was the miracle of the only other two hands in the house.

For hours, days, and weeks we played together in yellow light. I cannot even begin to think of what was in her mind during all this time, but in my mind there was suddenly a warm feeling of acceptance. I now no longer needed insects, maple seeds, Chinese glass balls, or mountains of lists to prove to myself I was still alive. And it was a very good feeling.

For years beyond count, the hands of the old woman had meant nothing, had had nothing to say and no one to say it to, had fussed about without reason. But now, and I knew this even though she never even once looked down at me for the whole time I was there, there was a purpose to her life. Whatever my hands and fingers did, after the days of our shyness had mostly worn off, hers would do also. When mine ran on the rug, hand on top of hand like Huns on horses, hers would do the same, both tight to each other and running from one end of a wooden arm to another and back again, and all of this with her eyes on the fire and never glancing down at me once. When mine flew in the air like planes piloted by Huns, hers would fly too, her eyes being the only other part of her that moved, though moving only in the several feet of space where the flames of my fire were burning. And whenever mine killed, which happened quite often, with one hand squeezing the life out of another like a Hun on the back of a Roman, hers would imitate mine either in the air like the birds I'm sure she remembered, or on the arms of her chair like animals, the trigger finger of her right hand always busy pulling pulling at targets even more imaginary than mine.

Sounds, too, were a part of our games once we lost our shyness and got to know each other better. Killing sounds mostly, Huns on horseback or in planes; a roaring and shooting sound from my mouth if planes, with my tongue clattering against my lips and teeth, or a deep and thundering earth-shaking sound from my throat if horses. And she, not having such talents, would do her best I think to make the sounds of birds in flight or deer running, her tight red mouth often forgetting to hum for minutes, and opening slightly at the height of my own noisy games, as if trying to say something, or trying to make again the blast of a shotgun, but emitting only a breath I could barely hear, and a thin dribble of white spit that her quick fingers would instantly erase, as if she too were afraid of being seen doing something silly.

Sometimes, however, we would seem to go too far, and because of my own tiredness and my worry about her, I would have to stop so that she could stop. I knew of the power I had over her, of the only touching upon another life that I had ever experienced, and I knew I had to be careful, for my sake as well as hers. I was good for her, I knew that, and I was also quite happy during most of these nights; but I never even for a second really thought that what I was doing was normal, or that my mind was thinking the way it should, and this began more and more to bother me very much. And on about the middle of my second month, I began to hear the sounds in my mind of a different kind of fighting: that between happiness and guilt. Guilt won of course, as guilt almost always does, and long before winter was over, I was back where I had started, afraid again, afraid of everything.

II

Winter one December night took hold of that house and shook it with a great white storm that lasted for hours. It was in the blackest of that night, right after a bad dream about hundreds of men who kept tumbling from horses, that the worst winter of my life began. On the afternoon before, the quiet gray air had been warm enough for thin coats and the still-unfrozen ground of the brown desert had been covered as usual with the balls of the slowly moving sagebrush that always followed the wind. But in the bright sun of the blue morning on the next day, and hours after winter had roared in under cover of blackness, I threw back my covers and went to the Jack Frost frozen windows and saw that all the old world was now gone, the balls of brown sagebrush now painted white and frozen to the crust of the deep snow for mile after shining mile.

It was on that night I think that I first began to be afraid of the entire world and not just of the people in it. My eyes were opened by a bad dream and for hours I stayed awake, not wanting that dream to come back, my mind and ears listening instead to a nightmare that was just beginning. At first I heard only the scamperings of the mice upstairs and within the walls of my room as they whispered their fears to each other, as they collected their autumn food and found safer places to hide in and then snuggled close to each other to listen to the low moaning of the rising wind. Then the whistling from one large mouth began, as if the first real wind of winter was laughing, and the creaking of the beams on the second floor as they too became afraid and began pulling at all those square iron nails that held the house together. Then all of the house began groaning, even though it had been through this many times before, and the glass of the cases in almost every room began scraping in their casings, like ice against wood. And with each minute the storm grew, strengthened by the fears that all small things have of big things, hitting against the house like some gigantic white animal whose hatred of me was much deeper than I had ever felt before. And in my warm bed under thick blankets I began to shake along with the house, something that I almost never did when alone, and I had to use every ounce of the energy in my mind and body not to do what I felt sure the storm wanted, not to go outside in pajamas and freeze to the snow like a ball of sagebrush. But there were worse things even than this. It was my eyes, those two most trusted parts of my mind and body, and what they saw for hours that frightened me most. There were no animals in my bedroom, no glass cases filled with fur or feathers or eyes staring at me, no chopped-off heads hanging on my walls, nothing to be afraid of in that way, only the hated rifles and shotguns lying in the wooden arms of the gunrack, and the rocks and arrow and spear heads that sat deep in the dust behind the two mountains of glass that were now trembling even more than me on both sides of my bed. But still, even though wide awake, I began to see on the walls of my room all the once-living things that I knew for a fact were in all the other rooms .... birds deep inside glass prisons moving their gray or white feathered heads, their orange or yellow beaks opening and closing in songs of pain .... and long and dangerous snakes, some as fat as my arm and others like fingers, diamond backs, sidewinders, whips and garters, all uncurling and crawling on dusty shelves .... and deer, or at least the heads of them, all with blood-red eyes, the many points of their antlers swaying in the dead air and scraping on walls .... and especially rabbits, dozens and hundreds of blue-eyed rabbits, each with the name of Jack and each with soft white ears that bent in the dead air of their glass prisons to point at me like fingers, as if it were I who had killed them and locked them up. I fought hard against this, telling myself over and over that I knew for an absolute fact that I couldn't really be seeing such things since I was in my room and they were in theirs. And I fought even harder against the shaking of my body, knowing from past experience that if I couldn't control it now, it might continue in school the next day. And then, during the worst of the storm, with half of my mind wanting to sleep because of what I was seeing and doing, and with the other half wanting just as desperately to stay awake because of the bad dream that I didn't want to dream again, I began to do both; I began for the first time in a long life to slip in and out of reality so fast that I couldn't tell the difference between the two. One minute the storm outside would be raging in my ears and telling me to die, and the animals and birds and snakes would be moving about and making the sounds of dying. And then in the next minute I would die just a little bit, and sleep and be in the old dream again, the same dream that had bothered me for years and would continue to hurt even long after I had grown up. First, I would see and hear animals, I would see houses shaking, I would wake up in my dream to the sounds of iron keys turning slowly in iron locks, and then wait quiet in the darkness while hoping and praying that maybe someone had made a mistake, and that the holder of the keys would leave my door alone. But it was never a mistake, never once, and I would watch that part of the darkness where I knew my door to be, and then always I would be blinded for seconds by the sudden yellow light of the hall as the door opened. Then blackness again, and a jingle-jangle sound of iron keys, and a tiptoeing of feet past my bed and into the room of the black table. And after a while, I would make myself be brave, and I would go into that room and peer around that black table with big eyes, like a Hun looking toward China, and I would look through another bedroom door that was always open to everyone in town but me, forever open night after night to all those ghosts wearing white sheets, like Romans in togas, and all of them forever standing in my dreams on heads to fight one another with their naked feet kicking in the smoky air. And almost always I would concentrate on my mother's long brown hair, loving the way it was wrapped around a pillow that always shone white like snow. But then, as always in this dream, the brown mane of that lion would shake, and I would hear for the thousandth time and sometimes even see again the glass of a bottle exploding on a bloody face, and hear again the sounds of screaming and the slamming of a door. Then I would go back to bed, or to sleep, dreaming a dream within a dream, remembering all that I'd seen and heard in that bedroom on all those nights before that bottle exploded, playing all I'd remembered over and over in my mind for hours, stopping only when the sun was singing at my window to tell me it was time to dress and go to school.

On the morning after the storm that began the worst winter of my life, I left my bed and looked through the Jack Frost windows, dressed and said good morning to the wooden Indian, ate a warm breakfast and bundled up as warmly as I could, said good-bye to my unhappy new parents who said good-bye back while staring at me strangely, and opened the front door to walk into the coldest of worlds.

Everywhere there was snow. I had never in my life seen so much snow. It was on and all around the house, in deep drifts at the corners where The Wanderer had fought especially hard to get to me, on all the tops of the black and white shingles in the garden, on the dirt road where my slow galoshes made hundreds of deep double footprints behind me, all over the garbage dump that was now as clean and white as the desert, and even on the Indian shacks, only the wood just beneath the roofs black now where all had been black only yesterday. But now yesterday was gone, the entire world had changed overnight into something different, and even though I was glad to see that certain dirty things were now clean, I was frightened and confused that the world could change so much in one night. For some reason I had forgotten what winter was like even though I had been through nine of them before. And to have all this happen in the desert, a part of the world that I had always thought to be hot and filled with salamanders and cactus, added so much to my confusion that I began to do something I had never done before. With each cold footstep I made an even stronger promise to myself that no matter how scared I was of talking to people, I would somehow find the courage at school to get one kid alone in the play-yard and ask him what the hell was going on. Question after carefully worded question formed in my mind and mouth with each step toward school. Over and over, and with the same preciseness that I had once used to make lists, I memorized the things I would say, doing my best to perfect the first sentence, and the second, and the third, all the way up to an entire conversation.

—Does this happen every winter? I would ask a boy after catching him alone in some bright corner. —Yes, I would say when he said it did. —Yes, well I never knew it snowed in the desert. —Yes, it snowed in Connecticut too, that's where I come from, it snowed there all the time, even in summer sometimes, but I don't remember too much about it.

But no, I can't say that, those sentences are silly, it never snows anywhere in the summer, go over the things to say, change them, make them right. But why am I worrying so much? People talk to people every day. And surely it won't be all that hard to go right up to one boy and start talking. Surely there'll be at least one standing way away from all the others. Perhaps one with a red coat standing by the fence. A small boy, it doesn't matter what grade he's in, and with pimples and a squeaky voice, and perhaps lonely too, even though he knows all about wintertime in the desert.

—I love the snow, I'll say to him after bumping into him by the fence where no one else is standing. —Last year, when I lived in Connecticut, it snowed like this, it snowed all winter long, does that happen here?

But what will the boy in the red coat by the fence do? What will he say to me, if anything, and just which one of my perfected sentences should I use next? Will he laugh at me? If he does, I suppose I must laugh back and then use another sentence. And what about my arms and hands, what should I do with them? Just let them hang down? But it's the first meeting that matters most. If I can get that right then perhaps all the other things will just happen normally and without any pain.

Yes, it's the going up to one that takes the most courage. Maybe I'll just walk over to the fence like any other kid and touch the sleeve of his red coat and smile and say—gee, it sure snows a lot around here doesn't it, does this happen every winter?

Everywhere there was snow. I had never before realized how many things it could cover. Even the stones in the cemetery wore white hats, even the roofs of the town that had been yellow or green only yesterday. And then, in the schoolyard, I got the biggest shock of all. On my way to school, while thinking up all those things to say, I had also spent a lot of my walking time imagining the way the schoolyard would look. But it didn't look that way at all. Instead of what my mind thought it would see and half-hoped it would find, dark and cold crouched children waiting alone or huddled in twos or threes by fences or close to brick walls, there was not even one single kid standing alone in a red coat. All of them, from the first graders up, were running and laughing and building things with the snow. Forts as tall as kids were being pulled from the ground and then defended with hundreds of flying snowballs. Armies of smiling snowmen were being raised everywhere. Faces reddened by the cold were rushing and laughing past me. The confusion was almost blinding. I walked deep into the yard where most of the kids were, something I had never had the courage to do before, and was hit several times by snowballs before learning how to duck. I walked around for a long time, mostly in back of the forts, staring hard at each happy face, my mind and mouth forming again and again the many sentences I had worked so hard on during my walk.

There were rocks in the eyes of the silent snowmen, the buttons in their white suits were made of pebbles, some had long red tongues hanging down that looked very much like the woolen caps of certain noisy girls I had seen being chased only yesterday, and most had long ears stuck in with black sticks broken and stolen from the silent trees of the orchard back of the football field.

I was walking freely in the very thickest of the enemy, and for the first time in this or any other school I saw I was now surrounded by kids who really couldn't have any feelings toward me either way since they were all too busy playing in the snow. I walked and I walked in this new freedom, it could have been fifteen miles or ten feet, I wouldn't have known the difference; and then I stood quite still in one spot, only my eyes and ears moving, and the bottoms of my galoshes that were peeling and smoothing the snow slippery beneath me. On my left there was a snowman three snowball stories high who hadn't yet been stuck with a mouth, but who wore two sticks for ears and one giant pine cone that was shoved in just below an acorn belly button. On my right there was a high thick fort, constantly being attacked and defended by hordes of screaming Huns throwing snow. I wiped my eyes, only partly to get rid of the white dust of the snowballs that were exploding all around me, and I did my best to stop the slight shaking of my body that was now, and for the first time since I could remember, being caused not by fear but by happiness. It worked. My mind had told my body to stop and my body had listened. I began to move my head slowly from side to side, thinking for a second of a small dark owl I had once seen sitting on a branch in Connecticut. Then I blinked my eyes and the owl disappeared. That too had worked. My head, with its two enormous eyes that sometimes blinked, was now moving about an inch an hour, though of course I had no way of measuring the speed. Not yet. As I was looking to the right, I could hear two voices from the left that were louder than all the others, and slowly my head began to turn in that direction. When finally I got there, I could see that now the snowman was wearing a blue scarf, and he was smiling at me with a long black stick that was broken upwards at both ends. I smiled back, past the brown bouncing head of a boy and through the yellow flying hair of a girl, smiled so wide it must have touched both ears. Then, on my right, I began to hear the loud sounds of a furious battle, and I turned my head toward that fort, which was now alive with attackers and defenders all jumping and crawling on and over the walls, and I found myself for the first time in my life actually staring directly into someone's eyes. He was a boy from the seventh grade with blue eyes, who was startled enough to pause for a second with his arm raised before catching his balance and continuing his attack on the fort. And that, I guess, is when it all really began.

I was invisible. There was no doubt about it. But then, the entire morning had been quite unusual. The sun was so bright it shone up from the land. All those noisy kids playing all around me were ten times happier than I had ever seen them before. This person in my body was standing among them and not being stared at, was more a part of the world than he had ever been before. And as I stood there, with my head continuing to move around slowly except for the several times when it had to duck quickly because of snowballs, and with my galoshes busy smoothing the snow beneath me into shiny wet ice, I began more and more and for the first time in my life to get that strange feeling of one hundred per cent happiness that I would only get again many years later when drinking or on drugs or during that first special hour that follows the release from a long jail term or when lying either naked or clothed beside another human being of either sex and any age whom I happened to like while at the same time knowing for an absolute fact that that person wouldn't suddenly get up and leave.

So there I stood in that schoolyard of loud shouts and happy screaming, drinking in all my new happiness like a hot sun melting snow. I was invisible. No one could see me. I could do anything I wanted. I could flap my arms and make the sounds of an owl. I could blow my nose if I wanted. I could kneel in the snow and look for insects and no one at all would notice. I could unzip my pants and pee hot yellow holes in the snow. I could take off all my clothes, even my underpants, and walk barefoot all over the yard and right in front of the prettiest of the girls. I could do all kinds of things and make all kinds of sounds, and no one would see or hear me. But then, and just as soon as I had made up my mind to do every single one of those things and perhaps a few more, I began to hear all around me the sounds of moaning. The front doors of the school were now being opened. At any minute the bell would begin ringing. A scream began in my stomach, shoved itself up through my chest, and puffed up my mouth gigantic with air. But just before my head had a chance to blow up and to pieces and completely apart, I saw her. She was a very little girl, either from the first or second grade, and she was sitting sad and alone in a bright red coat by a water fountain and picking up handfuls of snow with her gloves and then dumping them on her buried feet, just like a kid at a beach would do with sand. It was then, and at the same exact time that the loud golden bell rang, that I opened my mouth as wide as I could and screamed.

But of course no one heard me, for I was invisible, and besides, the bell was too loud, and after a couple of classes, I soon forgot I had done such a thing.

On that first day and for many winter days after, I sat quiet in hard brown chairs and waited and waited, but there was nothing. There was no talk of it, no mention of the snow. And except for the air raid–fire drills, it was just like that war in the Far East. Did they have to be actually in it to know it was there? Were the teachers embarrassed by winter? In the mornings I would watch with both eyes as the kids took off their coats and heavy galoshes in the hall while talking about other things such as the homework they had or hadn't done or the mothers and fathers of their lives that they loved or hated, but never of the weather or the war. Didn't they care about what was going on? Was I the only one? But there was nothing, no matter how hard and long I listened. In geography class, there would be talk of half-naked Africans sweating in the sun and running about with spears, which I know was a lie since it was too cold outside. In arithmetic, there were tests that I would fail and that had nothing whatever to do with the millions and trillions of tiny snowflakes that had fallen to turn brown sand dunes into white mountains. Language class was the same, with all the tenses that I could never get right . . . . the hot sun is burning; the hot sun has burned; the hot sun will continue to burn; the desert grasses are being burnt dry by the hot summer sun.

And even in the history classes that I liked so much, there was never any talk of reality, no talk of Huns flying in silver planes over frozen steppes. There was now no more talk of small rapid horses, even though I knew they were just as real now as when Miss Collingwood had first told us about them. Instead my favorite lesson had been changed, and my favorite teacher was a stranger. All her talk was about some man who had discovered the source of the Nile, had caught encephalitis from a fly called tsetse, and had melted one day while sleeping under the hot equatorial sun.

But where I was there was snow everywhere. After school that first day, while I was walking through the town toward the white desert, I had to shake my head often and put fingers in my ears to try to clean them out and hear better. It was the cars mostly, because always before they had made the loudest of sounds. But now the cars crawling past me weren't making the sounds they usually made, and their almost silent tires seemed to be turning only half as fast as my eyes saw them turn. Again and again in my mind I would try to hear the sounds of the cars and trucks and buses the way they had been before the snow. But it never worked. No matter how hard I tried, the reality of the almost silent traffic stayed with me. And it was the same with the people I passed. Their faces were as blank as they had always been, and their legs were carrying them past me as fast as always, but I couldn't hear their footsteps. I could hear my own loud and clear enough, stepping one after the other, crunching in the snow with a loud noise that reminded me of a dentist's pick filling one of my teeth. But I couldn't hear the footsteps of anybody else. Several times I stopped and stared straight ahead at some distant, snow-covered house, listening with all of my body each time some passer-by passed by leaving a touch of wind on my face or a smell of perfume or hair oil in the air. But never once a sound.

Perhaps even more than the quiet traffic or the people, the radios in the houses troubled me most. They all seemed to be turned much lower than usual, as if there was snow on them too, or as if their owners, embarrassed by bad weather reports and news of the war, had closed their evening windows tight so that the legs and minds of passers-by wouldn't tremble and worry too much and show to all the world that they were just as much afraid of the snow and the war as I was.

I began to read books for the first time in my life at fifteen in a small library I discovered one day on one of the many levels of my second insane asylum. *Robinson Crusoe* first, then *Alice in Wonderland, The Wizard of Oz, Forever Amber.* And then I found technical books. Those that explained the workings of the mind. Those of normal minds that had studied sick minds. And I learned many things. Mostly I learned, in that place of sickness where none of us ever spent more than five minutes with a doctor, that a little knowledge can be a thousand times more frustrating than knowing nothing about a problem at all. For instance, beginning at the age of ten and lasting for years, there were moments and sometimes whole days when my ears would stop working. And in that library I found a book on the psychological hearing problems of children, and very carefully read page after page after page on the causes of such deafness, none of which ever had anything to do with me.

What was I to make out of learning that the stirrup vibrates against the membrane that covers the oval window, thereby agitating the perilymph liquid in the inner ear, where the ossicles are held snugly articulated by means of a tiny muscle stretching from the eustachian tube, the muscle of which, the tensor tympani, connects to the anvil by means of a tendon, and through changes in its tonus prevents any loss in the transmission of sound through slackness in the bony system, which can be likened to a labyrinth hollowed out of the bony skeleton of the skull, a chamber within a chamber where the endolymph party floats in the perilymph and is sensitive to vibrations, sixteen thousand of these per second beating against a loud drum if you are normal . . . . or words something like that, words that of course meant nothing to me.

And I read lots of those books on the mind, all written in the same language, books that mentioned every one of my problems, but never once explained why I had them or how I could get rid of them, dozens of thick books that touched deep into excessive masturbation, constant rumination, compulsive counting and list-making, abnormal guilts and fears, schizophrenia, paranoia, rage, deafness, asthma . . . . none of which ever gave me anything but a headache. But enough of that tall skinny teenager reading big words in front of a wall-size two-way mirror where there was never anyone on the other side.

Some nights during that snowy winter of my tenth year that was the worst of my life, after remaking the fire in the old woman's room as loud and bright as I could make it, I would bring all my homework in and sit with it by the wheelchair, promising myself each time that this time I would really do all the work I had been assigned during the day. I would read the pages of the books that the chalk on the different blackboards had told me to read, and with my Eagle or Ticonderoga pencils and yellow notebook ready, I would struggle, sometimes bent over for hours in the yellow light, with the questions that always came on the last page of each assignment. But almost every single time I got to a question that I thought I might be able to answer, I would instantly forget everything I had just read. And so I would go over those pages again where I thought the answer might be and find that answer, but then instantly forget just which of the questions it was I had found the answer to. In my science book, for instance, I would find the meaning of a word, I would read that *bio* meant life and that *logy* meant the study of, and feel happy in the warmth of the fire and the knowledge that I knew two Greek words that a German had put together in 1802. And then I would turn to the page where the questions were, but see only those asking about amoebas and parameciums, and none at all on the Greek or German language.

I would almost always turn then to another book, each time glancing out of the left corners of my eyes at the old woman who would be doing her best to imitate me, flapping her hands over on one of the wooden arms of her chair, as if taking another book herself. The next one would perhaps be geography, and again I would slowly read each word of my assignment and study each map and then turn to the question page.

Question . . . . what is the most densely populated country in the world? Question . . . . which three countries produce and export the most coffee, rubber, zinc, and tin? Question . . . . which countries of the world have the hottest climate? . . . the coldest? . . . and which of these are the most productive in terms of steel output and human happiness?

And I, not knowing the answers to any of these, even though I had read them in words or on maps only minutes before, would turn back to all these pages, and find the answers again, but never once be able to keep them in my mind for a long enough time to connect them with a question and write them down, no matter how quickly either my hands or those of the old woman would turn in the air and slap hard at the problem. And then, perhaps, I would pick up the heavy arithmetic book and weigh it in my hands as the old woman did the same with the empty air, as if wishing that the meanings of all those endless numbers could somehow be picked up like a magnet and sent up through my arms and hunched shoulders and neck, all the way into my head that loved numbers but could never understand them. And then I would go on to something else, feeling the one in the chair beside me shrug her small shoulders at such nonsense.

Playing almost always came next after arithmetic, for there was never anything else to do. I would sigh, and then hear in the crackle of the flames the sigh of another person who loved me, and I would put my books to one side, as she pretended to do the same. Our hands would go slowly at first, as if feeling sad and guilty about all that homework that we just couldn't do. I would perhaps begin by scratching my fingernails on the rug, like the hooves of huge horses pawing hard in the dust, and then see and hear her own thin fingers as they rubbed on the wooden arms of her chair, as the small deer in her past had done before she had shot them. And little by little, in spite of my guilt over these games that was growing heavier in my mind each night, we would make our hands and fingers run and dance faster and faster, as if trying to burn them out like the logs in the fireplace, and as if we both somehow knew how little time we had left to talk and play and be together.

Sometimes, when the evenings were so cold that despite the fire I would have to keep on my coat, I would get up and put my fingers away and leave the fire and the humming, thickly bundled up old woman, and go out to the back porch and stand for a while with one arm on the logs and the other on an old icebox. And while breathing clouds of white smoke, I would watch the fire of the sun melting in the snow of the far mountains and the many-colored lights of the thousands of bottles in the dump a half-mile away going out one by one. And sometimes then I would see another miracle: I would see the cats.

At first only two or three would crawl across my eyes, then more and more until there were dozens, tiny black shapes barely moving on the white snow and among the piles of fresh garbage, some with eyes bright as bottles and all crawling low and careful in the black and white distance, like ants on and around piles of sugar, each slow shadow separated far from each other and all moving in one direction, as if pushed by the wind.

Then the windows of the Indian shacks far behind the cats would light up, and a gray smoke would begin rising from most of the tin chimneys, often with bright and quick sparks that looked like stars. And a door of a shack would open, light-ing that small part of the darkness for seconds before closing. Then another and another. No sound for a while. Only my breathing, and the fingers of one hand scratching on a log. And then a far-off war cry, and the throwing of rocks.

It was all a game, but an important lesson for me to learn about the hunters and the hunted. And I never would forget it. Only a very few cats ever got hit on those cold nights. I could tell by the sounds they made. And I guessed that they were always the slowest or the stupidest or the oldest, and therefore probably deserved to be clobbered and cooked and eaten.

An incredible amount of time later, when in my teens and twenties, and when finally it was my turn to play the part of the hunter, but with never a sunset behind me, and when as hungry as an Indian and hunting for drunk old men on the dark streets of countless cold cities, and when about to bash them from the shadows, or after having bashed them and ripped their pockets with can openers, or during the bloody act itself when they were crawling against a brick wall and screaming up at my heavy fists pounding up and down, I would often see again, jumping across my eyes and over the snow, all those cats playing games with starving people.

And now, as much as I don't want to, I must think and remember as much as I can of the madness in the winter of my tenth year that completely took hold of me one week and shook me as easily as a storm shakes a house.

12

It was in the week of the Christmas vacation that my asthma came back. I don't know why it chose to return just at a time when I was in so much trouble already, or just why, if it was caused by the fur of all those dead animals as I think it was, it had waited so long. But when it came, during the night and at first with a feeling of only the lightest of fingers around my throat, my memory of the third grade scared me so much that before an hour had gone by, I was terrified to find I could not breathe at all. Thereafter, during almost every hour of that Christmas week, ending only with the very moment that the doors on my first black station wagon were slammed shut and locked, I lived day and night in a kind of vacuum, as if someone had put a bag over my head. My being invisible helped some of course, since this time, unlike all those times in the third grade, and unlike all the future years of the teenager, no one could see my red eyes or hear my loud wheezing.

In the mornings, gasping for breath between sheets so wet I would sometimes think it had rained, I would leave my bad dreams and my bed and dress slowly and go into and through the long dark hall to the great wooden table in the dining room, and sit in my chair that was closest to the heat of the big iron stove in the kitchen. There, first saying a silent good morning to the wooden Indian and a spoken good morning to my new parents, I would eat my cereal or eggs and bacon and drink my milk while listening to the sawing of the termites in the cactus, the humming of the old woman two doors away who had just been fed her eggs and tea, and the wheezing of the adopted son.

After breakfast on most mornings, after first taking out the garbage that a noisy silver truck collected early each Thursday without ever saying thank you, I would leave the bad air of the house and walk as far as I could into the snowy desert, and come home only when it got too cold or my chest began hurting too much. Then, until lunch and for long hours afterward, I would spend most of my breathing time walking in and out of all those rooms of animals. Sometimes, after first making sure with my eyes and ears that no one could see or hear me, since my new parents were also on vacation all during this Christmas week, I would press my large open mouth on the cold glass of one or two of the prisons, and breathe words there with what little breath I could spare, my name mostly, and other words I had never told anyone before. And sometimes when I did this, I would see the miracle of my breath making clouds on the other side of the glass, but not very often. Also, on these long mornings and afternoons of trying my best to breathe, and again after first making sure there was no one around since I didn't really trust my invisibility all that much, I would often kneel down by the brown cactus and buzz back my name and other words in a language that only termites understood. Or I would go to the wooden Indian and stand or kneel while playing my hands slowly and carefully through the sharp silver wires of his raised hand and over the peeling red and blue paint of his arms, chest, legs, and wooden feathers. But never once did I ever dare touch that shiny glass of his angry black eyes.

At lunch and again during the suppers, I would sit as straight as I could with my new parents at the great wooden table, and do my best to eat correctly and without my hands shaking, all three of us always silent at these meals, all three of us munching and crunching, swallowing and staring into space, the only other sounds being the buzzing of the cactus, the humming of the old woman, and the wheezing of the adopted son.

It was also during this Christmas week that a thing stranger even than asthma would happen to me. I would be lying with eyes and mouth open in the darkness of my wet bed, or dressing, or trying to eat, or walking slowly in the bright morning desert, or talking to the glass or the cactus or the Indian, or watching the stoning of the cats, or sitting on the toilet, or doing any one of the many things that a person has to do for lack of anything better to do, when suddenly without any warning it would happen: my throat would open, I would finally be able to close my mouth and I would feel the miracle of the purest of oxygen rushing through my lips that had begged so hard and long for this, and my lungs filling fat with air. Where before there had been nothing, there was now everything. My chest would expand as big as a man's; my entire body would grow enormous, and so healthy and powerful that nothing would ever be able to hurt me again. Not asthma or homework or kids, not teachers or principals or adults of any kind, not storms or train rides or anything new and quick that shakes one's house, not anything in this world. All the things deep inside my body that had been so tense and heavy before, such as my heart and stomach, would relax. All the pounding and the pain would go away. All the once wooden-tight muscles of my arms and legs would soften and allow those limbs to move freely in the kind air like the smallest and lightest of the branches of a tree. My eyes and nose would dry up and not itch anymore; my skin would stop crawling with insects for minutes at a time.

But this was madness. Not to be able to breathe at all, and then suddenly to have all the breath I wanted; this surely is as close as I will ever come in my memory to explaining to myself just when and where and how it was that the worst of my madness really began.

It was while I was sitting by the old woman's chair one night that the most important of these many oxygen attacks hit me. My mouth was wide open toward the fire, as was the mouth of the old woman. The chest within my wet pajamas was thrown out as far as my dead lungs could push it. The two of us were rocking back and forth in the yellow heat of the fire, she silent in her chair against soft blue cushions, and me crouched on naked feet with my hands clasped hard on knees. And then it came. My throat opened, as if suddenly I had swallowed a piece of glass that had been stuck there for hours, my mouth closed, my body relaxed so quickly that I lost my balance and fell against the large wooden wheel beside me, and the miracle of the purest of oxygen began blowing through my brain. And then, and it only happened just this once in this week, I found myself doing something I had not done for a long time. I was crying. There was no doubt about it. Each time my fingers touched my face they came away wet. But it was not just this that made this particular attack so important. It was the old woman. For the first time in all our weeks together her head had turned away from the fire and was looking down at me, her wrinkled face now as wet with tears as mine. But it was not even that; it was a far better thing than all the miracles of my life put together. For it was during those next few minutes of breath that I somehow came to a decision that would stay with me all the rest of my life.

I would go way beyond the fighting I had begun so many weeks before in the summery autumn of my park when I had lived in new mother's apartment. I would fight a thousand times harder than I had ever fought before against all that was wrong with me. I would use much more than just hands and fingers and imagination, and I would kill many more things than just insects and maple seeds. I would begin, from these minutes of breath forward, to force the good part of my mind to become the stronger of the two, even if to do so I had to keep it working during every waking hour. And I would do my best to remember every single second of my life in which I breathed or could not breathe, and become a collector of myself the way some people collect animals or stamps. And I would compare each remembered second to each other every day for as long as I lived, continuously holding the best and the worst of my collection up to the light of sanity where they would shine like bottles, or like the eyes of cats, until finally the day would come when I understood what my life was about.

It was in the last days of my Christmas vacation that I made these promises to myself, and I knew that my fights had to be won before school began again. I didn't have much time. I couldn't walk into the schoolyard the way I was now, for I knew that no one who was shaking and breathing as hard as I was could stay invisible for long.

And so, determined now, and mostly quite calm inside in spite of the loud and painful wheezing breath that was shaking my body more each day, the good part of my mind was forever thinking and growing stronger. I would make it work while lying in the wet darkness of my bed, or while dressing or eating or walking in the desert or the house; and during almost every second of this time my mind was preparing for war.

I knew what war was. I heard about it all the time on the town radios, even though no one ever knew I was listening. War was giant iron tanks rumbling as loud as garbage trucks, or silver planes falling silent from clouds like birds after insects. I knew what war was. It was insects in the air, maple seeds on the ground, brown and green leaves floating on a pool of water. But it was pain and burning mostly. I knew that, though no one ever told me. It was everything my imagination could think of. It was Huns on small rapid horses riding through towns. It was a yellow siren screaming from the top of a City Hall. It was dogs barking, teachers getting excited, kids from all grades jumping up from chairs to hide beneath desks, kids marching single file through a hall to the snow to hear speeches on the horrors of Communism, smoke rising from parks and vacant lots, and the roar from the motors of silver ships as yellow men laughed. I knew what war was. War was my father when he had mailed his empty post cards from Oran and Casablanca and Naples to East Haven, Connecticut, and when, later, he had followed them home to die. I knew what war was. It was the shaking of a little wooden bridge somewhere, the burning of a library in Africa, hundreds of elephants freezing in the Alps, a message of Veni, Vidi, Vici written on a scrap of paper, a Thermopylae where the commander of thousands decides to fight in the shade, millions of Huns breaking through the Great Wall, splashing across the Danube, entering into golden cities . . . . and a desert town in Idaho where I was just as determined to win my war as anyone else in history.

I began to make lists on paper again, lists in the morning, lists while walking around the desert or the house, lists in front of the evening fire, but this time only of the things in life I feared most. But then I burned them all in the snow one day for fear someone might read them.

I began to use the good part of my mind as I had never used

it before, and quickly found that the more I thought, the easier it was to think. This new and strange feeling was, in some ways, almost as good as oxygen, and I began more and more to search out different ways in which to use it.

For instance, I would think of the way that one fifth grade teacher had taught us to use pencil and paper when dealing with a problem. First, find out and write down exactly what the problem is. Second, go over all the possible answers, no matter how silly some seem. Third, cross out and discard those that seem the silliest, and keep only those you think might work. Fourth, use a slow process of elimination, until only the best two or three are left. Fifth, use those two or three to attack that problem one by one until only one seems right; then discard all the others.

But as this so seldom worked, I soon discarded the whole thing and searched for better weapons.

Then there were all the assignments in my fifth grade books that I was supposed to complete during vacation. But all were just as meaningless to me in this week as they had been in the previous week. First, read the pages. Second, come to the question page. Third, answer all the questions. But whenever I found either of the two, I could never find the other; I could never connect anything on the last page with anything I had just read no matter how slowly and carefully my eyes had followed the words of the text, or how hard or many times my mind had worked when going over it again. Question . . . . what is the most important of the zinc- and tin-producing countries of our world? Question . . . . how does the lowly amoeba use the process of osmosis to enter so easily into other worlds? Question . . . . what were the three main causes of the Civil War? Question . . . . how can I breathe, stop shaking, become a better and more likable person, find the courage to talk to people, live a happier life; and all of this without textbooks or pencils or paper or outside help of any kind? Answer . . . . there is no answer. Answer . . . . there are no more answers to any of these now than there ever were. But there have to be answers. There must be. I just cannot believe that the entire world was made only for everyone else.

Every now and then when lying in wet darkness or walking in cold snow or through dead rooms, I would stop all other thoughts and force every muscle of my mind and body to concentrate only on one problem: I cannot breathe. I cannot breathe. My eyes would turn around in wet holes like the marbles of Chinese Checkers. The sharp glass of my memory would stab backward, stop, focus, and remember again all and anything in my past that might help me. A huge gray blimp seen floating far above some city somewhere. The many bunches of bright balloons I had once seen being filled by a man in a park with a wagon that hissed. Someone let go of one of those balloons and had cried, his wet noisy face lost far in the blue sky and never more than an inch away from that red dot, rising smaller and smaller until there was nothing. Or people puffing on cigarettes on the platform of a railroad station, or kids blowing thin green pipes into bubbles of all colors that explode into laughter, or brown paper bags being blown up and then popped by clapping hands, or the breasts of women, especially fat ones, which I thought were filled with air in the same way that the humps on a hot camel's back are filled with water and food, or of the wind in the desert when it blows whirlpools of snow in the air, or of the high freedom of the black eagles and chicken hawks when they rose and fell so comfortably in the blue desert distance of my winter sight, or of the many kites hanging from long white strings that I watched for hours one day while lying on my back in a yellow field somewhere, or of a summer bullfrog sitting fat on the shore of a black pond in Connecticut with his throat blown into a green balloon, or of the fish I had once found in the small hollow of a large rock at the seashore after the tide had forgotten all about him . . . . a puffer, I think it was called, and all puffed up and gray like a puffer should be, and prickly and scared and fat with the fear of being alone.

I would stop all other thoughts, every now and then, when lying in wet darkness or walking in cold snow or through dead rooms, and I would force every muscle of my mind and body to concentrate only on one problem: my body is shaking; I am being shaken to pieces by my body. My eyes would turn around and search inward. Even though at the same time I would want air, there is no air, there must not be. The tall yellow blades of the field grass in my memory must not shake, the red and blue irises of my past must not do more than sway, the leaves and branches of any tree must barely move, birds sitting in them must sit, the sun in the sky must stay where it is, and the water of my favorite black pond must sparkle in the light but never once be rippled by stones or air.

And for a while, unlike the times when I fought for breath, all of this would happen. Water spiders on black bent legs would drift lazily on top of their reflections among the webs of bright sparkles and dark shadows. Shadows of every shade of green would float, slow as the sun, across my pond and body. And my trembling would become less and less until you couldn't see it even if you looked. And the good part of my mind would sink deeper and deeper into those certain moments of my past which perhaps I had photographed and kept for just such a purpose.

Quiet things, and usually very small and helpless things, were what I thought about most. Mice and birds and the pets of small children. Sunlight, leaves, shadows on lawns or fields or water. The many things seen, touched, or listened to in gardens, woods, fields, or while sitting close to bright black ponds. Many giant memories brought from the back to the war front, hundreds of them, perhaps even more if I had ever taken a count. And each of these is filled with still more memories, all those I had once thought so worthy of saving I had kept them forever.

That small summer pond in the Connecticut woods was a giant memory. On its black muddy bottom, usually attached to the ends of broken sticks that were half in and half out of

the water, there were several strange things I had never seen
before, the most curious of white or green globs that moved in
my hands like jello whenever I reached in to pick them up. The
white was the prettiest. It held hundreds of tiny black eggs. And
whenever I held the white kind up to the sun, the white gelatin
all around the black eggs would shine silver. But the green was
the best, though it took a long time to figure out what was in it.
Inside the green jello there were hundreds of round white bubbles that looked like marbles, and within each of these, there
was a black tadpole waiting to be born. And some of them were
almost ready, I could see several making tiny movements whenever I held them high in the heat of the sun before letting them
all float down again to the very darkest of the bottom of the
pond.

But such nice memories never lasted very long. After thinking for a few minutes about blimps, balloons, kites, bubbles, and
puffers, the reality of not being able to breathe would have to be
faced again. There was never any other way. And I would find
myself fighting for breath even harder than before, but physically now, since my mind would be too exhausted to think any
further. And it was the same with shaking. After thinking for
as long as I could about small things that didn't shake, all those
memories too would begin quickly to disappear just when my
hopes were highest and no matter how hard I would tense all
my muscles and do my best to grab them back. And it would
be during these sudden reality-attacks that the bad part of my

mind would seem to take over more completely than ever before, as if it had been waiting patiently all this time for the good part to get tired.

My eyes would turn around again, in the night or the day, and begin staring at bad memories. A dog in Connecticut I had once seen choking on a bone. Another in the Idaho desert that was feeding on a dead body covered with flies. A vacuum we had once made in science class using a heavy bottle with a green snake inside and a black pump with a rubber handle that we all took turns at squeezing. All those memories of mice, in Boston I think, with their necks smashed in the kitchen traps that I used to look for each morning before breakfast. All those times I had stared at a hot oven while wondering how the animal inside would feel if all of a sudden he woke up. That gray puffer in the rock after some kids had used a stick to throw him to the sand where he began blowing himself fatter and fatter until finally that stick was shoved in to make him explode. All the balloons and brown bags and many-colored bubbles that I had ever seen in my life explode into nothing. Almost every single time in my life that my lungs had collapsed before, all of these remembered in tiny detail, each of these memories adding even more to the deadness of my lungs and mind and the shaking of my body. Those times in the third grade when I had fought against the pollen, the dust, and the stink of the shit. Those times when I had clawed at my school desk for many weeks. Those times in the backyard garden when I had fought against the flowers and carried them to my mouth, and when cousin Bobby had heard my choking and had come out to bring me back in. That time in Connecticut somewhere when I had watched a jackhammer shaking the man holding it into a blur. That great gray iron cement mixer I had watched for hours somewhere at some time of my life. An old drunk man sitting on a sidewalk in the shadow of a building somewhere, his bright red bottle shaking in the sun. A movie I had once seen in the auditorium of my fifth grade about farm animals and how those of us who lived on farms should always be on the lookout for hoof and mouth disease, lest we see again on our farms and ranches the following pictures that were taken in our Idaho county only a few years ago, those in color of hundreds of sheep, cattle, and horses all lying on the ground and choking and shaking horribly before being shot one by one by government men walking slowly among them, shooting and reloading and shooting as the farmers and ranchers watched quiet with their families behind fences, as the background music played louder and louder, as the feet of every kid began stomping on the bleachers until the entire auditorium was shaking, and as all our mouths opened wide to shout and boo loudly at the movie as our mouths were supposed to.

But in time, even those bad memories went away, though with never any help from me. And almost always then, after having struggled for many long minutes with all those thoughts both good and bad, my entire mind would suddenly become as empty of all thought as a vacant house. Several months before, when I had done my best in my school, park, and bed to think only of things being emptied, such as toilets flushed or marble bags spilled or matches blown out, so as to get rid of the way my mind was thinking, it had never worked for more than a few minutes at a time. But now, when I wasn't even trying, my exhausted mind would often remain empty for an hour or more, both the good and the bad parts, and the muscles and bones of my body would take over and continue the fight.

If I was in bed when this happened, my hands would grab mindlessly at wet sheets and covers and at the flesh of my body which I would later find to be spotted in many large places with blue and purple. Or if the shaking, or the reality of not being able to breathe, came back when I was walking in the snow of the desert, I would grab brown weeds or painful sagebrush or balls of snow that would harden almost into rocks in my fists. Or if it returned while I was walking through the rooms of the house, I would grab doorknobs, the intricately carved wood of tables and chairs, the air-bumps of wallpaper, the sharp wooden edges of glass cases, anything at all that might keep me from falling or shaking to pieces.

Sometimes, as I walked faster and faster each day through the many dead rooms of my mornings and afternoons, my hands and fingers seemed to become as strong as steel clasps, and welded so tightly for seconds to each thing I touched that all the blood drained. And then those white fingers turned numb, and everything they touched felt like soft feathers, and a pain would begin to travel up from my wrists through my arms. Whenever this happened, I had to stop and rest for a while because of the fear I had that that sharp pain might shoot all the way to my heart and kill me, another lesson learned from one of the movies in my school auditorium. And sometimes then I got dizzy, and my sight went away for long seconds, as if it were too busy pouring blood back toward my hands and fingers to be bothered with seeing.

But at these times I always fought harder than ever. I insisted upon seeing more than anything else. And then the darkness would slowly disappear, a red and then a pink light would filter through it and help me to see. But all this hard work always hurt my eyes, and everything I then saw would be changed, would be about half the size that my mind and eyes had remembered it to be. The once giant spinning wheel would now be a toy. The wooden Indian man would now be a boy as young as me. The glass cases, the heads on the walls, the lights on the ceiling, everything in the house, would now be shrunk in half and growing ever smaller as I stared. But even worse, each thing would appear to be losing its color. The brown wax face and red and blue feathers of the Indian would be draining of blood and becoming gray as the cactus, the once-brown cactus would now be as white as my fingers had been seconds before, and all the hated animals on the walls or inside the glass cases would be as pink and naked of hair as I was.

But no, above all else I could never allow such a thing. Color had always meant more to me than almost anything else, and this was the one thing I always had to bring back, this was the one thing in my life I would rather have died than lose. And again the good part of my mind would begin working. Again I would force it to think of things I had once seen to be filled or filling with air, and of a small black Connecticut pond filled with many miracles that were all very quiet. And with my mouth stretched wide open and my shoulders thrown back as far as possible, I would quiet my body as much as I could and stand still. And almost always then, my eyes would begin to see a miracle, and I would find that if I looked away from any one thing for a long enough time, that thing would get back its color and even begin growing again. I could see this all happening out of the grateful corners of my eyes. And when enough time had passed, always less than a minute I think, I could look back to each thing and see it again as I had remembered it to be, the same size and color and everything. The spinning wheel, the Indian, the heads on the walls. The dead animals that stared at me from the glass of each room once I continued my fast walking. Even the old woman, whose hands would now be running back and forth on the arms of her chair as fast as my legs. Even the dark faces of my new parents that I sometimes caught peeking at me from around corners. What a wonderful miracle. How beautiful it was to see.

But it was not always so easy to find a miracle. Sometimes, especially when sitting at the great wooden table, I would try so hard to defeat my various problems that there would seem to be enough energy floating inside me to power a battleship, and I would have to be careful not to explode into the plates of food; yet still there was never any breath or tasting of food, and my open mouth and shaking would often embarrass me so much that I would wish, and sometimes even pray, that I could explode, or at least become even more invisible than I was.

But there was one meal, my final one with my new parents though I didn't know that at the time, in which I suddenly found myself in the very middle of the greatest of all my miracles.

My hard-working mind had done its best to force my body as stiff as if it were dead. Even the fingers on my knees had stopped, all of them now as damp with sweat and as numb as the rest of me. Even the lips of my open mouth, so chapped from all these days of begging for breath they were cracking with pain, softened when I thought of soft things floating on water, and the pain went away. In my mind there were good memories, then bad, then none at all, as my mind became empty of all thought. And again, because of the war and the blood pouring back toward the white steel clasps of my fingers, my eyes saw nothing but blackness, and I had to fight hard to bring sight back. And when sight came, there was again a shrinking of things, and a draining of color, and then more and even fiercer fighting. And both the size and the color of each thing did come back, as they always did. The yellow and black of the large plates and bowls of antique china. The thick brown of the gravy and green of the vegetables. The bright silver color of the silver. The many different colors of the clothes, hands, and sad faces of my new parents. But then, during this last meal with them, there was one other thing that came back.

Sound. Suddenly my ears explode with reality. The thick wax of my plugged-up ears melts and flows happily down both sides of my neck like warm sweat. Sound. My ears are now alive again after a long time in which I had been too busy with other problems to notice they were dead. Sound. My eyes are going crazy trying to find out where all the new and different sounds are coming from. I hear the howling of a cat. My heart pounds in my gigantic chest. The buzzing of the brown corner cactus is as loud as if a hive of wasps had just been broken in half on the table. The old woman two doors away is humming on both sides of my head. The sounds of my wheezing which I had forgotten about, seem as loud as many horses after a long run. My head snaps back and I stare at the high ceiling. Mice as large as elephants are thundering through all those empty rooms above. The lights where I stare burn like torches held in the dark by thousands of waiting Huns. I can hear the wind. I can hear the shuffling of the feet of armies. And now, I can hear shouting.

—Pass the potatoes, please. Thank you. Pass the peas, please. Thank you. Would you like to have some gravy?

My head falls from the ceiling. My new parents are looking at me. His black-haired muscled arms are resting on the table, his enormous eyes are as black as those of the wooden Indian.

She repeats her question, her thin white arms are extended toward me, her small brown eyes are filled with promise. But
what can I say to either, what is there to say to this woman who
is speaking to me for the first time in days and holding a dripping dish toward me, only inches away from the battlefield?
What more can I do that I've never done before? My eyes stare
at all the brown spots exploding on the white tablecloth. My
mind thinks so hard on this new problem that my stuffed-up
nose can almost smell burning. Then she puts the dish down
with the roar of a cannon and my head snaps back to the ceiling.

—He's much worse today, she says.

—I know, but it will all be over soon, he says.

—Did you see how he left the bathroom this morning?

My head falls, snaps back again and again. The bathroom?
What bathroom? Oh yes, I remember now. That bathroom. But
there were smells and noises in there I had to stop. Surely they
can forgive me for such a small thing.

—Yes, I saw, he says.

—He's not human, not anything we ever talked about. . . .

—They were not human, my history teacher used to tell us.
—They were like animals on top of animals, practically welded
to their small rapid horses. They ate, drank, and sometimes even
slept on horseback. They were a race of centaurs. They often
rode in waves for days without stopping, a hundred miles in
one day sometimes. Nothing could stop them, not the Great
Wall of China, not the Holy Roman Empire, not even the

---

forces of the West that waited beyond the mighty Danube. At night, once their horses had collapsed, they slept on the hard ground of whatever they had conquered that day, with their heads resting against their sheep or goatskin saddles. But before they slept, each first always tied around his left wrist a short rope of horsehair which was attached to the one long rope behind him where all the horses were tied. And if, on any of those many cold nights, any one horse ever heard the sound of an approaching enemy, it would pull on the long rope and alert all the other horses which in turn would wake the Huns who would all jump up with their right hands on their weapons, ready to do battle.

—Don't worry about it, you'll make yourself sick by worrying so much, he says. —I already told you, there's a room available, the papers are signed, the nightmare will be over by Christmas.

But that's it. That's the greatest of all my miracles. What a wonderful thing to suddenly find out. My new parents have decided that the nightmare will be over by Christmas.

Oh, how I used to love Christmas. Cousin Bobby coming in my room in pajamas. A red sled with sharp silver runners. A bow and arrow set with a big stand-up target. Some puzzles to put together and take apart. Many tin toy soldiers. And a tree growing inside, actually growing in a pot of water right inside the house. And with white cotton at the bottom where Bobby had put many tiny houses. And with lots of silver angel hair, pretty glass bulbs, and lights of more colors than even Bobby could paint.

—They were especially fascinated by things bright and colorful. They had lived all their lives on the gray and barren steppes of what is now called Siberia, a cold and cruel land where the flowers of summer blossomed and died in one week, and where babies often fell even before the flowers. And so it was no wonder they reached for golden cities. But they weren't human, they were animals. Whenever they found those cities, they destroyed them. And on the nights before holidays, they didn't think at all about what we would think of; they huddled close on the cold ground and thought about each other. And like animals, they loved their children and were very kind to them. But also like animals, they were easily frightened by any sudden change around them or within the tribe. If, for example, some member of the tribe was suddenly discovered to have a disease, the word would spread quickly; there would be a silent gathering of rocks, and the one who was sick would be chased to the wilderness to die. But we must forgive them for that, for it was the only way the tribe could survive. But on their many travels they did sometimes pick up more than rocks and swords. Over the years, ever so slowly, useless gods and ancient superstitions died, and the Huns began more and more to be conquered by the customs of each people they conquered.

Confident now that the movie about the end of the Second World War being shown in the auditorium to the lower classes is and will be much louder than any of her records, the history teacher in my memory plugs in the record player she had brought to school on the day before Christmas vacation, even though she knows, as we all know, that the principal does not approve of such things. And then, barely above the sounds of the atomic bombs exploding far down the hall, she plays her records while telling us about some of the great battles of history. The Marseillaise is first, then Meadowland, Peat Bog Soldiers, the 1812 Overture . . . . and then finally and full blast, and only partly because, as she explains, it has in it real bells, eighteenth-century bronze cannons, twelve-pound howitzers, French and British muskets, and the drumming sound of thousands of running horses, the most magnificent thing I had ever heard in my life . . . . Beethoven's Wellington's Victory. . . .

Confident now that all my fighting has been worth it, that whatever my madness does now is okay since by Christmas the nightmare will be over, and that now there is very little time left in which to fight and win every one of my battles before school begins again, I do what I have never dared to do before: I let go all the terrible Huns of my mind and body, and I declare total war.

My heart pounds in my ears like drums. My hands fly through the air and drop down hard again and again like bombs from planes. Now it is the table's turn to shake. Silverware jangles in plates and against glasses like church bells. The gravy dish spills over. It doesn't matter. Each time something is knocked over or spilled, my new parents jump a little in their chairs, their brown or black eyes rising to the ceiling, their long arms reaching out to mop up or fix things right. The butter dish falls over. No matter. Both my mind and body are now free to do whatever they want, at least until Christmas comes because then the nightmare will be over. White worms thick as fingers crawl in and out of the meat. The small horses of my rapid fingers are running and fighting for the last time. I hear horns and howitzers and muskets. My throat opens a little, my cracking lips close halfway and I can taste the flowing of blood. My eyes are now able for the first time ever to look all the way across the great wooden table without fear. I am happier now than I have ever been in my life. And won't the kids at school be surprised when I walk right up to them and start talking. I am winning. Dear God, I am winning. My new parents now have a son. They are cleaning their mouths with small white cloths. I don't want to remember anymore.